M. M. Bello

Six Years Later

AF205000

M. M. Bello

Six Years Later

A Contemporary Novel

JustFiction Edition

Impressum/Imprint (nur für Deutschland/only for Germany)
Bibliografische Information der Deutschen Nationalbibliothek: Die Deutsche Nationalbibliothek verzeichnet diese Publikation in der Deutschen Nationalbibliografie; detaillierte bibliografische Daten sind im Internet über http://dnb.d-nb.de abrufbar.
Alle in diesem Buch genannten Marken und Produktnamen unterliegen warenzeichen-, marken- oder patentrechtlichem Schutz bzw. sind Warenzeichen oder eingetragene Warenzeichen der jeweiligen Inhaber. Die Wiedergabe von Marken, Produktnamen, Gebrauchsnamen, Handelsnamen, Warenbezeichnungen u.s.w. in diesem Werk berechtigt auch ohne besondere Kennzeichnung nicht zu der Annahme, dass solche Namen im Sinne der Warenzeichen- und Markenschutzgesetzgebung als frei zu betrachten wären und daher von jedermann benutzt werden dürften.

Coverbild: www.ingimage.com

Verlag: JustFiction! Edition ist ein Imprint der
LAP LAMBERT Academic Publishing GmbH & Co. KG
Heinrich-Böcking-Str. 6-8, 66121 Saarbrücken, Deutschland
Telefon +49 681 37 20 310, Telefax +49 681 37 20 310-9
Email: info@justfiction-edition.com

Herstellung in Deutschland:
Schaltungsdienst Lange o.H.G., Berlin
Books on Demand GmbH, Norderstedt
Reha GmbH, Saarbrücken
Amazon Distribution GmbH, Leipzig
ISBN: 978-3-8454-4535-9

Imprint (only for USA, GB)
Bibliographic information published by the Deutsche Nationalbibliothek: The Deutsche Nationalbibliothek lists this publication in the Deutsche Nationalbibliografie; detailed bibliographic data are available in the Internet at http://dnb.d-nb.de.
Any brand names and product names mentioned in this book are subject to trademark, brand or patent protection and are trademarks or registered trademarks of their respective holders. The use of brand names, product names, common names, trade names, product descriptions etc. even without a particular marking in this works is in no way to be construed to mean that such names may be regarded as unrestricted in respect of trademark and brand protection legislation and could thus be used by anyone.

Cover image: www.ingimage.com

Publisher: JustFiction! Edition
is an imprint of the publishing house
LAP LAMBERT Academic Publishing GmbH & Co. KG
Heinrich-Böcking-Str. 6-8, 66121 Saarbrücken, Germany
Phone +49 681 37 20 310, Fax +49 681 37 20 310-9
Email: info@justfiction-edition.com

Printed in the U.S.A.
Printed in the U.K. by (see last page)
ISBN: 978-3-8454-4535-9

"How did you find me?"

"Told you, I was walking around the park enjoying this beautiful day and then bam, there you were sitting on a bench?"

Katherine raised an eye brow.

Todd sighed. "I went to the shop and your secretary told me where to find you."

Katherine's eyebrows drew together in a slight frown. Janine knew better than to do that-although Katherine was somewhat glad that she did.

As if reading her thoughts, Todd said quickly. "I pried it out of her. The poor thing didn't stand a chance. What can I say, I'm good at what I do."

"What is that exactly? Prying information out of helpless secretaries?"

He grinned. "That's only for emergencies."

"And seeing me was an emergency?"

"Oh yeah, big one."

Katherine couldn't help the smile that formed at her lips. The man was impossible; he was making it hard not to like him. "I see," Katherine said looking straight ahead.

"I'm a lawyer, actually."

"Oh."

"What? You don't like lawyers?"

"One of my closest friend's a lawyer," she said referring to Josh.

"Right. Well, now that we've gotten that out of the way...what time do you want me to pick you up?"

Katherine twisted in her chair to look at him, eyes flashing. Todd smiled. At least now he had her attention. "I told you I don't think this is a good idea."

"Why?"Todd's eyes bore into hers.

"Maybe I'm not interested." Her voice sounded cool and indifferent even to her ears. She averted her eyes once more.

He studied her profile for a few seconds. He could tell that she was holding her breath. "I don't think so," he whispered in her ear.

1

2

*To my dear sisters for believing, pushing
and urging me on....*

4

Chapter One

Katherine Johnson glanced at her watch and sighed. *There's no way I'm going to finish this tonight*, she thought frustrated. She wasn't looking forward to attending the charity gala her friend's parents were having at The Plaza tonight. She wished that she could get out of it, but she knew that her friend Josh would never forgive her if she did.

Katherine and Josh's fathers had attended Yale together and later went on to establish their first company together, an advertising agency. The two of them made a great team and the company raked in millions within its first five years. Eventually, they discovered their own business niches and had gone on to pursue other things. Katherine's father had gone on to build a real estate empire while Josh's father ventured into pharmaceuticals.

Growing up, their families had spent a lot of summers together. As kids, Katherine and Josh had never gotten along. Katherine had found him irritating and he thought she stuck up and snotty. By the time they got to junior high, Katherine had grown immune to Josh's incessant teasing and he had got used to her ignoring him. They got paired up as lab partners in the eighth grade and had been friends ever since.

Katherine glanced at the floor plans she'd been working on once more. *I still have about thirty minutes. I'll just go through one more.* She skimmed through the extravagant requests of a bride-to-be and began to sketch, letting her imagination add layers of creativity to specifications before her. A small smile formed on her lips as her hand flew across the blank page. Although, Katherine's love life was in shambles, she didn't mind planning weddings. In fact, she loved it.

When Katherine decided that she would close down her prosperous floral shop in Paris and move back to New York to set up an event planning outfit, she knew that she was taking a big risk. Running a floral shop and an event decorating outfit was no easy feat, especially in a place like New York.

Even though Katherine had been optimistic, she never dreamed that it would take off as fast as it did. Her family's connections had guaranteed her a steady stream of clients. More clients than she could handle. Katherine found herself juggling so many jobs she barely had time for herself. Not that she minded the distraction; it was exactly what she had in mind when she moved back to New York.

"Ugh!" she groaned when she heard the shrill sound of the door bell. "Now what?!"

She opened the door to find her best friend Ashley Van der Camp tapping her foot impatiently. Ashley looked stunning in a black floor length Versace gown with a plunging neckline. Her red hair was swept up in an elegant up-do and her makeup was immaculate. Katherine and Ashley had been best friends for as far back as she can remember.

The Van derCamps's New York town house was near the Johnson's. Their mothers had been good friends and when Ashley's mother died of cancer when she was five, Ashley who never got on with her step mother, had practically moved in with the Johnson's. Her step mother hadn't minded. She never like kids anyway.

Despite their different personalities and interests, growing up Katherine and Ashley were inseparable. Katherine was calm, loved school and spending time at home while Ashley was vivacious, boy-crazy and loved to shop.

After high school, Katherine had moved to Europe to attend college while Ashley, despite her father's protests, had gone into modeling. Between modeling jobs, Ashley would visit Katherine and force her to take her clubbing. As much as Katherine looked forward to seeing her friend, it seemed like every time Ashley showed up at her doorstep all dressed up, it was to drag her shopping or to a party she was not interested in attending. And today was no different.

"You're not wearing that are you?"Ashley asked making a face at the white shift dress her friend was wearing.

"What are you doing here? I thought you were going with Alex?"

"His name is Alessandro," Ashley corrected dreamily. "I ditched him. I thought, my best friend would be better company."

Katherine folded her arms across her chest, raising a perfectly shaped brow. She knew Ashley too well to know that that was unlikely.

"Don't worry about Alessandro dear, he will meet us there," her friend added hastily.

"Did Josh send you to get me?" Katherine asked.

Ashley laughed guiltily as she pushed past her friend into the spacious living room.

"I knew it." Katherine slammed the front door. "He's driving me nuts. He's called me five times already. I swear he 's up to something," Katherine said as she made her way back to the study.

"Where are you going?"

"To my study to finish my sketches."

"Oh, no you don't." Ashley ran to stand in front of Kate. "Josh will kill me if you're late."

"We won't be. Trust me, I'm as good as ready." She had already taken a shower and done her make-up, all she needed was to slip into a dress and she would be good to go.

"Not from where I'm standing."

Knowing that she would not be able to get anything done with Ashley hovering over her, she decided that she might as well get dressed. With a sigh Katherine went to the bedroom heading to her large walk in closet.

6

Katherine loved her closet it was one of the reasons she had bought the apartment. The fact that its location was ideal, or that it had an extra bedroom, a study and a spacious living area with a great view made the apartment stand out from the other ones she had seen. But it was the closet that had been the deciding factor. She wasn't surprised when the realtor told her that a former model used to live there and had gotten the closet remodeled before moving in.

The closet was almost as large as the living room of her apartment in Paris. It had a safe as well as an island with little compartments for accessories, watches and jewelry. There were several full length mirrors as well comfortable seating. One wall was covered with shoe racks and shelves for handbags and had the most elegant ladder she had ever seen for reaching the higher shelves. Katherine's first thought when she saw them was that she would never get around to filling the shelves. Unlike most of her friends, she had never been an avid shopper, but a few shopping sprees with her Ashley and she was almost there.

Katherine leafed through the numerous designer dressers hanging in closet and pulled out a simple black dress with a demure neckline.

"You're kidding me right?!" Ashley exclaimed as Kate laid the dress on her bed.

"What's wrong with it?"

"Come on Kate, you're not going to a funeral."

Fuming Kate returned the dress to her closet and came back with a strapless teal dress. "That's what I'm talking about. He is so going to love you in that."

"He who?" Katherine's eyes narrowed suspiciously.

"Um.. Josh didn't tell you...?" Ashley started uncomfortably.

"Didn't tell me what?"

Ashley turned away form the mirror where she had been admiring herself. "Okay, you have to promise you won't get mad..."

"Promise."

"And you'll go to the gala."

"Just tell me," Katherine demanded exasperated.

"Fine," her friend came to sit on the edge of the bed her eyes dancing with excitement. "Josh's college buddy, Todd is going to be there and ...."

Katherine picked up her dress and started to return it to the closet. "I'm not going."

"Come on, you gave him your word," Ashley said scurrying behind her.

"He lied so that's a moot point," she retorted as she hung the dress back up.

"Well, you gave Josh's parents your word so you're going." Ashley grabbed the dress and shoved it t at her best friend. The phone rang. "That's probably Josh. You know that he's just going to keep calling you all night. And even if you do manage to ignore him tonight, you won't be able to ignore him forever. He'll call you a chicken till the day you die."

Ashley had a point. Josh could be so annoying, sometimes it was easier to just give in to his whims. It seemed like josh had been trying to set her up with one of his numerous friends ever since she got back. He simply did not want to accept the fact that she was not interested in dating anyone and wouldn't be for a while.

So far, Katherine had managed to weasel her way out off his plans to "get together with some old friends for drinks". Katherine had hoped that he would get bored and let it go, but no. Her resistance seemed to fuel his determination. His latest candidate was his college buddy. Todd Jenkins. "I've known Todd for almost ten years. He's a great guy. You'll like him," Josh kept saying.

To Katherine's chagrin, it seemed that Todd was just as reluctant to meet her as she was to meet him. She had heard Josh's phone conversation with Todd. Although she couldn't make out what Todd was saying, it was apparent that he had very little interest in attending the benefit or meeting Katherine. "I don't want some guy being nice to me just because Josh told him to. You know how pathetic that makes me look."

"You're anything but pathetic. Boring maybe, but certainly not pathetic." Ashley said walking back to mirror to pat her hair. "Besides, you just have to show up. If you don't like the guy, you can just bail and that'll be the end of it."

Katherine sighed. As much as she hated being put on the spot, Katherine couldn't bear to disappoint Josh's parents besides her parent would be there. Her mother had already started complaining that she was working too hard. She didn't want her thinking she was right. "Fine. I'm only going because I promised Josh's parents that I would. But I'm not staying."

"You might if you knew what Todd looked like," Ashley said with a knowing smile. She continued to pat her perfectly coiffed hair. "I've met him all I have to say is ... yumm."

"If he's so great, how come you're not dating him?" she asked as she slipped into her dress.

"I don't think I'm his type," Ashley said making a face. Ashley was used to having men fawn over her, and Todd's complete lack of interest in her had been a bruise to her ego.

"Yeah, and I am," she retorted her voice dripping with sarcasm. Since when did guys turn down girls like Ashley for girls like her? Ashley had not been featured in vogue twice for her personality. She has a beauty that

8

was almost ethereal. Even though she'd given up modeling she still got calls from her agent. "Anyway, I don't want to hear a word about Todd or whatever his name is," Katherine huffed as she struggled with the zipper of her dress.

Ashley laughed. "Fine, just hurry up and get dressed." She zipped her friend up and went to the closet to choose shoes for her.

Ashley chatted excitedly about the new guy she'd been seeing throughout the ride to the hotel. Alessandro, an Argentinean polo player had visited her art gallery to buy a painting and it has been instant attraction. "Oh Katey, I think he just might be the one."Ashley enthused even though they'd only been together for two weeks.

Katherine rolled her eyes. Ashley fell in love so easily. After a few great dates she'd start dreaming of happily ever after. Unfortunately, happily-ever-after always came too soon. The guy would either turn out to be married or a toxic bachelor and Ashley would crumble into a bundle of tears. Fortunately, Ashley fell out of love as easily as she fell in love. After a month of moping around, she'd met someone new and life would be a bed of roses once more.

Katherine wished she had her friend's resilience. It had been almost a year since she and Greg had gone their separate ways and she was still one big heap of misery. She felt much older than her 28 years and was certain that she would die an old maid.

Her three year relationship with Greg had come to an abrupt halt when he was transferred to Dubai. Katherine had been so excited about the promotion. They went apartment hunting in Dubai together-something Katherine saw as a sign that Greg was finally willing to settle down and plant some roots. She waited for Greg to ask her to move to Dubai with him but the invitation never came.

It wasn't until she confronted him that she realized that he had no intention to include her in his future plans. In a tortured expression, Greg told her that he hadn't felt a connection in a very long time and that he had fallen in love with someone else. Katherine was crushed to later discover that Greg had been falling in and out of love all over Paris throughout their three- year relationship and her heart was not the only broken heart he had left when he moved to Dubai.

Greg had been everything she thought she wanted. Ten years her senior, Greg seemed more mature and sophisticated than anyone she had ever dated. He was handsome, smart, refined, came from a good family and he was exciting.

Katherine fell hard and fast. Before she knew it they had practically moved in together. She gave him the keys to her apartment and created room for him in her closet. She didn't mind his erratic working hours or the last minute business trips because when they were together he always made her feel like she was the only girl in the world.

It wasn't he had moved to Dubai, did she force herself to face the tell-tale signs that had been there all along-the late hours, the unexplained business trips and the fact he had keys to her apartment but she didn't have the keys to his. Katherine felt like such a fool for believing that he preferred her smaller, cozier apartment to his ultra-modern pent house. Paris became unbearably lonely for her so she sold her shop and moved back to New York to try and pick up the pieces of her life.

Although her business was thriving after little more than a year, her life felt empty. She wasn't entirely sure if she was really over Greg and she certainly wasn't ready to start dating again. Until now, she'd managed to avoid her friends' attempts to get her "back in the saddle". *Maybe I'll just hire someone to pretend to be my boyfriend. That would get everyone off my back.* Katherine thought with a smile. The smile quickly turned into a frown when she realized that, having a fake boyfriend would mean that she would have to spend a certain amount of time with him and she couldn't imagine anything worse. I guess they'll just have to endure seeing me attend events stag for another year or ... ten, she said to herself bitterly.

Chapter Two

"Why did I ever agree to get involved with this?" Todd muttered under his breath.

One reason. Because he never could say no to his best friend Josh. Josh had a knack for getting his way. He knew exactly which buttons to push to get exactly what he wanted.

Josh and Todd became friends in college. They started out as study-buddies but soon became very close. By the time they graduated from college, Todd and josh were inseparable. They shared even an apartment in law school.

Although both of them were fiercely competitive, they never let it get in the way of their friendship; instead it made their friendship stronger. Josh had a quick mind the ability to absorb a large amount of information in a short amount of time; that, his sense of humor and his gift of persuasion made him every teacher's dream.

Todd on the other hand, had always been more of a slow-and –steady-wins the-race type of guy. What he lacked in brains, he made up for in diligence, determination and passion. And Todd was passionate about the law. At first, it had been a case of him trying to emulate his father.

His father had been passionate about his work and would speak of the law and the constitution with some sort of reverence. But the more Todd studied and understood the law, the more he thirsted for it and the more he realized that he didn't want to be a lawyer just because his father had been a lawyer. He wanted to be lawyer because he believed in the law and in justice.

After law school, it was Josh's parents who had put in a good word for him at Campbell and Scotts, a prestigious law firm. Although he enjoyed his internship at the state prosecutor's office and had considered working there after law school, he knew that working in a law firm like Campbell and Scotts was an opportunity of a life time for someone like him.

The week after they graduated from law school, Josh's parents asked Todd what his plans were. Still looking for a job, Todd told them that he was thinking of accepting the job offer at the state prosecutor's office. He had learned a lot during his internship there and had actually enjoyed it.

"Why would a bright young man like you, want to end up in a place like that?!"Josh's father had asked incredulously. "Believe me son," he said putting an arm on Todd's shoulder and dropping his voice, "you'll just end up over-worked, unpaid and burned out in a couple of years." Giving Todd one of his penetrating stares, he asked, "Are you thinking of going into politics? Is that what this is about?"

Todd stared at the man. Up until now, he had never considered being anything other than a lawyer. "No, sir," he said. "I just want to be a lawyer. A good one."

"Good," said the older after a while. After dinner, Josh's father handed him a business card with the name Alvin Campbell printed on it. "Go see Al first thing Monday morning. Tell him I sent you."

Todd did just that. He liked Al immediately. The 65 year old was considered a bit of a maverick in the courtroom and as unpredictable as the weather, but he was also fair and supportive. He told Todd that he was creating a job opening for him as a personal favor to Josh's dad, but Todd would still have to go through a preliminary interview and a two week probation period during which he had to prove that he "talk the talk".

The other partner, Benjamin Scott was on the phone when Alvin took Todd to his office. Benjamin Scott motioned Todd to pick up a large pile of case files. "Go through them and tell me what you think, "he said and dismissed Todd. Todd buried himself in the case files. And two weeks later, he was hired. Grateful for the opportunity, Todd continued to work as though he were still on probation.

The hard work had paid off. At 29, Todd was now regarded as a major asset to the firm. He knew that at the pace he was going he was likely to make partner in a couple of years. Making partner was all Todd thought about. He ignored his friend's jabs at him being a bore and tried to avoid his friend's attempts to hook him up. He didn't see the point of dating anymore.

Most of the girls in Josh's circle were clones of each other-rich, spoilt and they all looked at him like he was a piece of meat. Of course, once every blue moon he'd hit it off with a girl, but after a couple of weeks-he would get an acute feeling that something was missing.

Todd wasn't afraid of commitment, he was just afraid of committing to the wrong person. Having grown up without a family, Todd knew exactly what he wanted. He wanted someone real, someone with substance, someone he could share his life with and have a family of his own with. He was also sure that he wasn't ready for that-not now. Right now all he wanted was to make partner. He sighed when he thought about the briefs he had been hoping to go over tonight.

"Cheer up, man," Josh said as they stepped into the banquet hall. "You look like you're headed to your execution."

"Sure feels like it."

"Trust me Katherine is different. You'll l love her," Josh assured him with a tap on the back.

"Sure that was what you said about all the girls you ever tried to set me up with."

Todd could not believe that that he'd let his friend talk him into yet another blind date. He tugged helplessly at the bow tie that was choking him as he took in his beautiful surroundings. The elegant ballroom was packed with round, white-draped tables with beautifully arranged flower centre pieces. Women in shimmery cocktail dresses dripping with diamonds floated around the room with their equally elegant dates.

His eyes swept the room again, trying to guess which of the reed thin socialites Josh was trying to hook him up with this time. That was when he spotted her.

She stood about eight feet away from him looking like she'd rather be somewhere else. Now this is definitely different, he said to himself as he took in her generous curves. She wasn't a tall stick figure like most of the women there. She was petite and perfectly formed. The strapless dress she was wearing accentuated her tiny waist and full bottom before flaring out. Her thick blond hair fell in soft waves past her shoulders giving her a wildly seductive tumbled out-of-bed look.

Her unapproachable, out-of-place demeanor piqued his interest. This girl wasn't laughing it up with her girl friends or turning this way and that to make sure her diamonds were showed to their greatest flashy advantage. In fact, she looked exactly how he felt. Bored and irritated.

Todd's breath caught in his throat as the woman suddenly turned around and looked straight at him. He was aware that he was staring and that it was rude to stare to do so but he couldn't tear eyes away from her creamy skin, full lips or her green eyes. His heart beat quickened as her eyes bore into his. He can't remember the last time a woman made him feel this way.

He was absorbed with his desire to make partner that he rarely thought about dating or anything else for that matter. Occasionally he would hook up with someone and they would see each other for a couple weeks till it fizzled out and they would both go their separate. But it had been a while since he'd done that either. Josh was right, he definitely needed to get out more.

An evening with a girl like that would definitely be more entertaining than an evening going through briefs, he thought with a smile. He saw something flicker in her eyes before she quickly shifted her gaze.

"There you are," he heard Josh say. He turned reluctantly to see a beautiful red head in a tight black dress coming their way with a big smile on her face. There was something familiar about her but he couldn't quite put his finger on it. Even though she was good looking enough to stop traffic, Todd couldn't help wishing it had been the petite that josh was hooking him up with not her. Granted both women were elegant but the petite woman's beauty looked more laid back and effortless. Everything about her seemed natural and sultry and unrestrained.

"Hello, darling," the red head said kissing josh on both cheeks. "Hi, you look great, but then what else is new?"

She laughed. "You don't look too bad either."

"Thanks," Josh answered with chuckle.

"Hello," she greeted Todd with familiarity.

"Hello," Todd answered trying to remember whether they had met before. Todd felt slightly uncomfortable at her obvious appraisal of him. Then it came back to him. She had given him a similar same look when they met

13

her at an art exhibition with Josh, only then it seemed to have more of a come-hither effect to it. "It's good to see you, again," he said slightly relieved that this wasn't who Josh was trying to hook him up with. Although she seemed friendly enough, she looked like a lot of work.

"Where's Katherine?" josh asked.

"She was right behind me," Ashley said looking around. "Oh, there she is. Excuse me."

Todd couldn't believe his stroke of luck when he saw Ashley walk up to a small group of people. Please let it be the girl, he prayed silently. His prayers were answered as he watched the girl excuse herself and follow Ashley. He noticed that her jaw was clenched and her fists were balled up at her sides her. With her slightly flushed cheeks and flashing eyes, she looked almost... angry. But that only added to her appeal. Todd's heart was pounding against his chest so hard he was sure Josh could hear it. He inhaled sharply.

Josh smiled. "Told you she was different," muttered under his breath.

"Hello, Katey," Josh said with a big smile.

"Hello Josh." she all but glared at him.

"Katherine, this is Todd. Todd Katherine," Josh said jovially seemingly oblivious to the deadly looks was giving.

Her eyes widened slightly when she turned to look at Todd. "Hello," they both said at the same time. She was even more beautiful and dainty up close. He noticed that even with the high heels she was sure she had on, her head barely reached his chin. But she lacked in height, she more than made up for in character. Standing there glowering at the two friends who stood a head above her, she looked intimidating.

"Darling I'd better go look for my date," Ashley said quickly after an uncomfortable silence.

"Yeah, me too," Josh said quickly, grinning widely.

"But you didn't come here with anyone," Todd pointed out.

"I know," Josh said wagging his eyes brows. With his long lean build, honey blond hair and large brown eyes, Josh was a magnet for the ladies. They liked him and he sure liked them! With a not-so-subtle wink, Josh took Ashley's arm and the two of them disappeared into the crowd.

Katherine scowled as she watched Josh walk away with a triumphant look on his face. She felt like strangling him. She hated being put on the spot and that was exactly what Josh was doing! Although he was half-way across the room, Katherine knew that Josh would be spying on them all night to see if they hit it off, not to mention her parents. She didn't miss the knowing smiles her parents and Ashley had exchanged. It seemed as though everyone was in on the let's-not –let-Katherine-turn-into-an-old-maid mission.

14

Gritting her teeth she turned towards her date. They sure aren't taking any prisoners tonight, she said to herself as she glanced at the tall, dark handsome stranger. Where did they find this guy? Tall, dark, handsome stranger... ugh! How cliché! But even as she formed the thought, a part of her couldn't help thinking that there was nothing cliché about this guy.

To say that Todd was not what Katherine had expected was the understatement of the century. When Ashley had told her that she was going to be hooked up with one of josh's friends, Katherine had expected him to be the generic Wall Street types. She had not imagined anything like those shoulders, the bulked-up chest straining against the fabric of his tux, the thick wavy dark hair that was in a slight need of a trim.

When she'd caught him watching her she had been startled by the hypnotic effect his smoldering eyes had on her. Now this is a man that can sweep me off my feet, she had thought. Then she remembered that it had been like that with Greg in the beginning. Lust at first sight. She had been fascinated by his good looks and charm almost instantly. Not to mention that gorgeous English accent of his. She had thrown caution to the wind and given in to her impulses and look at where it got her. She was not about to put herself through that again.

"Would you like a drink?" he asked gesturing to the waiter carrying the champagne flutes.

Katherine nodded annoyed with herself as she tried to ignore the warmth radiating from his body when he leaned toward her. As Katherine took the champagne glass from Todd, their finger brushed sending a jolt of electricity whizzing through her entire body causing her to almost drop the glass. *This would have been so much easier if he were unattractive. Five seconds and he's got me hyperventilating like some simpering teenager!*

Katherine sipped her champagne in silence.

"Josh tells me you guys grew up together," Todd said attempting to break the awkward silence.

"Yes, we did."

"He tells me that you're a florist."

"You could say that, yes."

"He tells me that you just moved back here from Europe."

"Yes, I moved back last year." This is beginning to feel like a cross-examination, Katherine thought, Occupational hazard, I'm sure.

"And how has that been?"

"It's a nice change," she said after a beat.

"Definitely a nice change," Todd didn't realize he said it out loud till he caught her puzzled look. "I mean from

Paris and the French."

"That wasn't what you meant, was it?"

Todd scratched his head ear. "Ah no."

"So what did you mean?"

"You sure you wanna know?"

"I was just being polite but now I am curious."

"Curious? That is a good sign. For a second there I thought I was boring you," Todd said with a smile.

Katherine smiled back when she realized that he had just given her the perfect opening. "Not at all. It is just that it's a work night and I have been here all day setting up."

"You did the place up?" Todd asked incredulously.

"Yes, I did," Katherine said lifting her chin not sure she liked the surprise in his voice.

"You did an amazing job," his expression close to awe.

"Thank you," Katherine said coolly trying to ignore the warm feeling his compliment had evoked. She noticed that people were starting to take their places at the tables. *This is my cue.* "I'm actually pretty exhausted. I think I'll just call it a night. It was nice meeting you, Todd," she said extending a hand.

Todd took her hand in his immediately. Katherine noticed that the hand was darkly tanned, strong, with neat blunt fingernails and not a hint of kept-man elegance she was accustomed to seeing. They looked like a worker's hands. He continued to hold her hand and Katherine found herself drowning in the most beautiful pair of blue eyes she had ever seen.

"Do you really have to go?" he asked softly

Katherine nodded.

"Won't the host be disappointed to see you leave so soon? "

"They already know that I wouldn't be staying long."

"And you're sure it has nothing to do with the company?" he asked in a teasing voice, but Katherine could sense the effort he was putting to sound nonchalant.

"Absolutely nothing." She smiled.

"In that case, let me at least escort you," he smiled, his hand tightening slightly around hers, sending warm tingling feeling shooting up her arm.

Katherine bit her lower lip. As physically drawn to him as she was, Katherine knew better than to take up with a man like him, a man who probably couldn't keep it in his pants, a man like Greg. This was one road she wasn't going down again. It took more than a little restraint to pull her hand out of his. "I'm a big girl, I can find my way, thanks." Handing him the champagne flute, she spun on her heel and headed out the door leaving Todd gaping after.

She was barely out the door when he caught up with her. "Look, I have the feeling we've gotten off on the wrong foot somehow. I'd really like to go sit down somewhere, not as part of our 'date' but just so I can thank you for actually showing up."

Katherine threw him an impatient look and then glanced at the door way.

"You did say that the company wasn't that bad," he reminded her. "Or were you just being polite?"

"Yes," Katherine said. "I mean, no.... "

"Well then prove it. Have a drink with me."

"Oh, come on," he urged when he saw her hesitate. "I'm one of the good guys here. Honest."

The man simply would not get the hint. It was infuriating. Just say no. You've done it before, to countless of guys... better-looking guys, guys with gorgeous European accents and titles to go with it, guys with better breeding and nicer haircuts, she told herself. Just say no. Instead, she found herself saying, "Fine, just one drink."

Katherine told herself that it was the polite thing to do. It had nothing to do with the way he filled his tux, or the dark wavy hair that made you want to run your fingers through or the earnest look those piercing blue eyes were giving her. She was just being nice. That was it!

"Great," he said visibly relieved. "We could go to the hotel bar. I'm sure you wouldn't mind getting away from that crowd," he added disdainfully.

Tired of the mindless chatter, Katherine was more than ready to get away from "that" crowd. It just wasn't her scene. Sure she had the money and family connections to fit in perfectly with the crème de la crème of New York, but she preferred not to.

After spending so much time in Europe she was pretty sure that she had very little in common with most of her childhood friends anymore-except for Josh and Ashley. They had somehow managed to avoid the shallowness and ennui that plagued everyone else in their social circle. Usually, Katherine could stand the company of New York socialites in small doses, but tonight was not one of those days. Tonight she just wasn't in the mood to socialize.

17

Katherine let Todd led her through the hotel lobby to a cozy but almost empty restaurant. As she settled into her chair, Katherine tried to ignore the tingling sensation on the place at the small of her back where his hand had been.

She was surprised when Todd ordered a club soda with ice. She had noticed earlier that he had turned down champagne earlier opting for a non alcoholic cocktail instead. It wasn't often that a man who was clearly sober declined champagne at a party and ordered a non-alcoholic cocktail. In Manhattan, it usually meant one thing: addict. Of, course, Katherine mused, there had to be something wrong with the guy. He's an alcoholic!

"Don't worry, I'm not an alcoholic or anything."

Katherine reddened, embarrassed that he guessed the direction of her thoughts. Taking in the dark hair and thick eyebrows she thought, maybe he's half middle-eastern. "Muslim?"

He laughed. "No."

"Monk?"

"Wrong again," he said laughing. He could tell that now she was being sarcastic. A hot girl with a sense of humor-he didn't know they made them like that anymore.

She looked at him expectantly.

"I just prefer to keep a clear head at all times," he said with a shrug. "You know one of those people that have very *very* low tolerance for alcohol. That's me. It's embarrassing really. Had a few incidents in college and I have never really recovered."

"I think we've all had incidents in college."

"You too? No!" he said in mock horror leaning closer.

"They do have beer bongs in Europe too, you know."

"I didn't know that."

"See? You learn something new everyday."

Todd chuckled. Beautiful and funny! Nice! He thought.

Drinks turned into meal as Todd and Katherine exchanged funny stories growing up. Katherine laughed more than she had in the past six months. To her surprise, she had gone from trying to get rid of him to actually flirting with him. *Is that what I am doing? Am I actually flirting?* Katherine couldn't tell. All she knew was that she was having a good time. The evening was perfect except for the text messages Ashley kept sending her to make sure that she was really okay. Katherine sighed when her phone vibrated again.

18

"Is everything alright? Your phone's been vibrating all night." Todd asked his voice full of concern.

"It's Ashley. I'm sure her date feels like smashing her phone right now."

"*I* feel like smashing her phone right now!" Todd growled.

Katherine laughed. "She's just curious," she said.

"I noticed and so is josh, but he only texted me once to find out why we weren't in there." He smiled ruefully. "You see, now I can go back with my head held high coz I got the girl."

"You didn't actually get the girl," Katherine pointed out.

"Yeah, but you're still here. That counts for something."

Katherine regarded him coolly. "Actually, I was just leaving." She reached for her purse and made to get up.

"Wait," Todd shot out of his seat, alarmed.

"Got you!" Katherine sat back down laughing.

"That wasn't very nice," Todd said laughing and feeling more than a little embarrassed *So much for playing it cool.*

"I know." She smiled. "I couldn't help it. You kind of asked for it though," she added unable to keep the trill of amused laughter from escaping her lips. Their eyes met and held.

Katherine noticed the way his jaw flexed and his eyes narrowed, shining with dark intensity and appreciation, all traces of that easygoing good humor disappearing as he settled back into his chair. Her laughter died as the atmosphere surrounding them changed, crackling with tension. She had never been as physically aware of anyone as she was of him at that very moment. Not even Greg.

Katherine tore her gaze away from his and glanced at her watch. She had to leave and leave now while she still had the strength to do so. "I'm sorry, but it's getting late and I really do have to get going."

There was no doubt in Todd's mind that Katherine was attracted to him. He could tell from the way she looked at him, or rather tried not to look at him. There was also no doubt in his mind that their evening was about to end, judging from the determined expression on her face. At least, he got to spend time with her. He knew better than to push his luck.

He knew that she was as opposed to the idea of being set up as he was. Hell, it looked like she would have liked nothing better than to plummet Josh to ground but some where between "hello" and "drinks", she had changed her mind. They both had.

Todd was more than glad he had agreed to attend the banquet. And to think that he had been putting off meeting her for the past couple of weeks! The most important thing is that they've finally met and they like each other or at the very least are attracted to each other. Not a bad start. Maybe it was time he jumped back in the dating scene.

Todd gave her a sad smile that tugged at her heart strings. He didn't want the evening to end anymore than she did. Without saying a word, he dropped a few bills on the table and rose to pull out her chair.

They walked out of the hotel and waited for a cab in silence. "It was nice meeting you, Todd," she said when a cab pulled up.

"Thank you for staying, I had a great time."

Katherine smiled and nodded, not quite meeting his gaze. Not a good sign.

"I'd like to see you again." He said holding on to her elbow to keep her from disappearing into the cab.

Their eyes locked and the protests died on her lips.

"Please say yes," he murmured. "For no other reason than that you want to." He tried to keep his voice light, but his eyes were intense and the air crackled between them.

Katherine bit her bottom lip. She wanted to yes. She was surprise how much she wanted to. He seemed like a nice guy. His eyes were warm and friendly and he had a laid back sex-appeal. *And* he made her laugh. It would be so easy to fall for him and that scared her. "I don't think it's a good idea," she said shaking him off.

"I do." Todd watched as she slid into the back seat of the cab gracefully. "I'll find you," he promised.

"I'd rather you didn't," she said and shut the door.

Liar! He thought as he watched the cab till it disappeared from view. "Cab sir?" the hotel bellman said.

Todd shook his head and started slowly down the street replaying the evening in his head. Smiling, he made a mental note to thank Josh fro dragging him out tonight. Katherine was definitely one of a kind and there was no way in hell that he was staying away from her.

Chapter Three

"Do you come here often?"

Katherine looked up in surprise. She had escaped to the park to get away from the shop as she often did when the weather was nice. She loved New York in the Spring when everything went from gray to green and the flowers blossomed. She would find a secluded spot and settle down for about an hour enjoying the beauty and tranquility, letting her imagination run wild. She had come up with many new concepts at this very spot. No matter how troubled she was, she could always find peace of mind at her spot-except for today.

It had been five days since the night of the banquet, but as hard as she tried, Katherine couldn't stop herself from thinking about him. She thought about him when she was at work, in the shower, when she went running ... she just couldn't seem to get him out of her mind. And now there he was walking toward her nonchalantly.

"Do you?" she retorted surprised at how aloof she sounded. He looked better than she remembered. His pin-stripped dark blue suit brought out his eyes and he looked more relaxed with loosened tie and the first two buttons of his shirt undone. His hair looked like he'd spent the entire morning running his hands through it. Instead of looking messy, he looked sexy as he smiled down at her.

Katherine's question seemed to throw him off balance. "I...no. Hardly. I guess I'm just having a rare case of spring fever." He said with a smile. "Happens." He sat down at the opposite side of the bench and looked at her, obviously pleased with himself. "You don't mind if I join you do you?"

"You already have," she pointed out. "How did you find me?"

"Told you, I was walking around the park enjoying this beautiful day and then bam, there you were sitting on a bench?"

Katherine raised an eye brow.

Todd sighed. "I went to the shop and your secretary told me where to find you."

Katherine's eyebrows drew together in a slight frown. Janine knew better than to do that-although Katherine was somewhat glad that she did.

As if reading her thoughts, Todd said quickly. "I pried it out of her. The poor thing didn't stand a chance. What can I say, I'm good at what I do."

"What is that exactly? Prying information out of helpless secretaries?"

He grinned. "That's only for emergencies."

"And seeing me was an emergency?"

21

"Oh yeah, big one."

Katherine couldn't help the smile that formed at her lips. The man was impossible; he was making it hard not to like him. "I see," Katherine said looking straight ahead.

"I'm a lawyer, actually."

"Oh."

"What? You don't like lawyers?"

"One of my closest friend's a lawyer," she said referring to Josh.

"Right. Well, now that we've gotten that out of the way...what time do you want me to pick you up?"

Katherine twisted in her chair to look at him, eyes flashing. Todd smiled. At least now he had her attention. "I told you I don't think this is a good idea."

"Why?"Todd's eyes bore into hers.

"Maybe I'm not interested." Her voice sounded cool and indifferent even to her ears. She averted her eyes once more.

He studied her profile for a few seconds. He could tell that she was holding her breath. "I don't think so," he whispered in her ear.

"What? Now you're a mind-reader." Katherine snapped at him.

"Actually, now that you mention it..."he scooted towards her closing the distance between them and picked up her hand placing it in his with her palm turned up. Using his index fingers he traced the lines in the palm of her hand. His hands were warm and strong, like the first night they met.

She mustered the courage to look him in the eye for the second time. His chest was huge and strong. Her gaze travelled to his tanned neck corded with muscles and then to strong jaw which jutted out in determination. Although his face was freshly shaved, it displayed a hint of swarthiness that would provide the most delicious frission of roughness when it grazed against her cheeks. She let her eyes linger on his sensual lips and before clashing with his startling blue eyes.

He held onto her hand firmly as she started to pull away. Every nerve-ending in her body was like a live wire. Katherine held her breath. She felt like she was being hypnotized as Todd looked into her eyes while he trace patterns on the palm of her hand. Her blood roared in her veins at the feel of that strong, warm touch. She was completely incapable of stopping the visual images that flooded her mind.

"I can see that you're interested. Very interested. I can also see that you don't trust me." His fingers hovered

22

over her hand. "Katherine, just say yes, we could be good together. I feel it and I know you feel it too," Todd said softly his warm breath fanning her face. Katherine swallowed. It would be so easy to give in to him to give in to this, but at what price?

Katherine laughed bitterly pulling her hand away. She straightened reaching for her purse. "Todd, you're right. You really *are* good at what you do."

"Good bye Todd," she said as she walked away leaving Todd speechless.

Todd walked back to his office slowly, feeling very dejected and very foolish. "We could be good together... I know you feel it too" Todd cringed as he recalled it. Even to him, that sounded like a line. A cheesy one at that! Of course Katherine wasn't going to fall for a cheesy line like that. Way to go Casanova. Things were going great before he got cocky.

Sitting on the park bench in her navy blue silk wrap-around dress, black sling-back heels her hair pulled back in a bun, note-book and pen in hand a look of concentration on her face she looked so beautiful, he wanted to just stand there and watch her. And he did. He stood there drinking in the sight of her before he approached her. The blue dress she was wearing looked great against her skin and brought her eyes.

When he sat next to her, he had to will himself not to brush the loose strand that had escape from her bun. Not only did he love the way she looked, he loved her wit and sense of humor. He wasn't sure if she had been happy to see him or not. Her face was so hard to read. One thing was for sure though. She was physically drawn to him. That she couldn't hide. He could see her fighting it.

It was obvious that she didn't trust him. He would have to take things slow. He would have to find a way to get her to lower her guard; that is the only way they would have a chance. The next time he saw her things would be different. He would try to keep his attraction under reigns. It would probably take all of his self control and a lot more patience than he possessed but he would do it because she was worth it.

Katherine was distracted for the rest of the day. Her brain refused to function properly and kept going back to the way it felt when Todd took her hand in his. She knew that she wasn't going to get enough sleep that night. She was right. She woke up in the middle of the night, her legs tangled in the sheets. Frustrated. The next morning she had her secretary book her an appointment with her masseuse. She needed to unwind.

By Friday, Katherine felt brave enough to go to the park on her lunch break. It had been three days since she'd last seen him and was sure that she would be able to handle herself better now. She half-expected to find him sitting on her bench smiling. I guess he got the point she thought with a twinge of disappointment. She sat on the bench with a sigh and closed her eyes letting her imagination run free, trying to think of a new concept for a wedding shower she was working on.

Occasionally, Todd's face would pop up and she would quickly squash it. An hour later, Katherine got up and

23

walked back to her shop with a bounce in her step and a deep sense of accomplishment. She has figured it out. The solution to her Todd-issue was simple: keep busy.

She would have lunch with Josh, and go shopping with Ashley on Saturday, spend Sunday with her parents and it would be back to work on Monday. She had a wedding to pull off in less than two weeks, that should keep her busy and out of trouble!

"You never did tell me how things went with Todd," Josh said to Katherine as they settled down in a garden bench after a game of tennis.

"What do you want to know?" her voice sounded calm even though her insides were wrecking havoc. She was glad she was wearing her sunglasses.

"You're not going to do that too are you?"

"What?"

"Shut me out. When I asked him he said fine and wouldn't say anything else."

"There you go, it was fine."

"I was just so sure you two would hit it off you know," Josh said sounding genuinely disappointed.

"Why?"Katherine asked curious. "Because *he's* bored and *I* need a new boyfriend."

Josh laughed. "Kind of." Katherine threw the towel that had been hanging around her shoulder at him. He ducked before it hit him in the face. "But seriously," Josh said pushing his sun glasses to the top of his head, leaning towards her, hi s expression serious, "Todd is a good guy, I just thought you might welcome the change."

"What change?"

"Dating a nice guy, for one thing"

"Todd being the good guy, I suppose," Katherine said drily.

"He's a hell of a lot better for you than that bastard ever was," Josh said between clenched teeth. To say that Josh hated Greg was an understatement. He'd been against the relationship from the very beginning, telling Katherine that Greg was bad news. Katherine had been blindly in love and had ignored her friend's warnings.

Not wanting to talk about Greg or Todd, Katherine smiled. "That's not much of an accomplishment. I mean you can't get much lower than Greg."

Josh laughed leaning back in his chair. "I suppose you're right."

Katherine and Josh had lunch at the club, catching up on events of the week. Sensing that Katherine didn't want to talk about Todd, Josh stayed away from the topic only mentioning that Todd would be out of town for a week and he would need a running buddy. Katherine gladly took up the offer.

Chapter Four

Katherine walked around her friend's art gallery slowly. "What do you think?" Ashley asked.

"I think tonight is going to be a good night." Katherine's gaze swept across the room. The place looked great. The brilliant white walls and the perfect lighting complemented the bright canvases as did the large structure that looked like a tree bark in the middle of the room. "It's a full house."

"It is. I meant what do you think of the artist's work?"

"They're certainly interesting," she responded. She knew that it had taken her friend months and a lot of convincing to get the artist to display his work at her gallery. Hearing people ohhing and ahhing, Katherine couldn't understand what all the hu-ha was about. It looked like a five year old had been playing with crayons on the canvas. She couldn't imagine paying thousands of dollars for any of the paintings hanging in the gallery.

"Aren't they though? He paints with such wild abandon. There's so much depth and emotion to his work. You can almost feel his pain." Ashley said gazing at one of the paintings.

"Mmm," Katherine replied nodding. All she saw a disfigured person-she couldn't tell whether it was a man or a woman against some bluish blackish scribbles. If there was any depth to the colorful mess before her, Katherine missed it. To her, it just looked like the artist did the painting when he was drunk, dead drunk. All the same, her friend deserved her support. "You did a good job finding him, I'm sure you'll be sold out be the end of the night," she said giving her friend an affectionate squeeze.

"That's the plan," Ashley replied with a wink. Despite her carefree attitude, Ashley was very dedicated to her work. She had surprised everyone when she announced that she would give up her modeling and go back to college. Her father, who never thought of modeling as a career was ecstatic. He gave Ashley the keys to a huge building the day she graduated from college and offered to help her set up her gallery every step of the way.

Although, Ashley wanted to make it on her on, she eventually caved in. Fortunately, her father backed off the minute the gallery was up and running, letting her take the reins. Having been a model for almost five years, Ashley welcomed the change of pace and the independence that came with working for herself. She loved discovering new talent and bringing out the best in them. She also loved the feeling of euphoria that came over her every time she made a big sale. Judging from the ambience, she sensed that tonight was going to be a very good night.

"Hey did Nicole and Steve come together?" Ashley asked tilting her head slightly towards the door.

Katherine stole a glance towards the door and then sighed. "No, I think so." Katherine wished that Nicole would stop throwing herself all over her brother. It had been going on for so long, it was almost too painful to watch.

"They look kinda cute together though, don't you think?"

"Mmm." Katherine had to admit the long legged Nicole with her dark hair and aquamarine eyes and Steve with his athletic build, honey blonde hair and soft brown eyes looked like they were made for each other. She wasn't surprised to see Nicole batting her eye lashes at her brother.

Katherine and Nicole had known each other since they were in grade school and Nicole had been in love with her brother for almost that long. What she was surprised to see was that her brother was actually flirting back!

Men, she thought bitterly. Five minutes ago he was going on and on about the girl he'd been seeing and now here he was trying to hook up with someone else. Never mind that Nicole had just gotten out of an ugly relationship and was probably very vulnerable. Never mind that Nicole was one of her closest friends. As much as she loved her brother, she didn't want to see Nicole get hurt. She knew what it was like to get your heart trampled on by the man you love. "I hope he's not leading her on."

"No, Steve wouldn't do that. He's probably just being nice, I'm sure Nicole knows that," Ashley reassured her. "Besides didn't you say that Nicole was seeing someone and it was serious?"

"You're right," Katherine responded guiltily, squashing the treacherous thought from her head. Katherine and her brother had always been close. Three years her senior, Steve had always been protective of his little sister and understood her in a way nobody ever did. It was Steve who had fought tooth and nail with their parents to let her go to college in Europe.

When she said she wanted to open her floral shop in Paris, Steve had taken a break from his private medical practice and flown in to Paris supported her. It was Steve she called when things had gone sour with Greg. Steve had gotten on the earliest flight he could went to straight to Greg's apartment gave him a black eye before going to pick up the pieces of what was left of his sister.

To Katherine, Steve had always been her hero. She remembered crying her eyes out when Steve enlisted in the army after 9-11. It took a long time to come to terms with the fact that her brother felt the need to put his life at risk, to help keep America safe.

She later understood that that was a part of who he was. Steve was a good guy. Although her brother was a bit of a lady's man, to his credit, he has always been upfront and honest with all the women he had been with. Deep down she knew that her brother would never lead a girl on, especially if that girl was her friend.

"Come here, I wanna show you this painting. It is my favorite." Katherine let her friend drag her across the room. "What do you think?"

"It's really something," she said. The truth was, she wasn't entirely sure what to think. "Where is the man of the hour anyway?"

Ashley all but rolled her eyes. "He wouldn't come."

"Couldn't or wouldn't?"

"Wouldn't!"

"What artist misses his art show? Unless he's dead, that is"

"That was what I said. I told him that the critics would want to meet him and we'd sell more if he came, but he wouldn't budge. Anyway, I was lucky enough to get him to display his work."

"Maybe he's camera shy."

Ashley sniffed. "Trust me, shyness has nothing to do with it. He's just conceited, that's what he is."

"Speaking of critics…" Katherine cut in before Ashley launched into another tirade on the elusive painter.

"I'll be right back," Ashley whispered to her friend and moved toward the well-known critic as he admired another one the paintings. Like Ashley, he too looked impressed.

Katherine gazed at the painting before her trying to find the meaning that was so clear to Ashley and everyone else. She had to admit there was something sad about the painting, but other than that it looked like a bunch of scribbles to her. "Yeah, I don't get it either," an amused voice came from behind her.

Katherine froze, there was no mistaking who the sexy baritone belonged to. She felt goose bumps form all over as her heart began to beat a mile minute. She glanced at Todd who was now standing by her side. "Maybe you just don't understand modern art," she said coolly looking at the painting. She couldn't allow herself to look at him. Standing so close to him that she could feel warmth radiating off him and smell his cologne was almost too overwhelming for her.

"What's there to understand? A man gets drunk and goes crazy with a bunch of crayons and then *we* get drunk and go crazy about *his* crazy drawings. I don't know about you, but that sounds a little crazy to me."

Katherine laughed. "Well, that's one way to look at it."

"No, that's the only way to look at it," he said laughing with her.

"We're here to appreciate the artist's work, not make fun of it," Katherine said trying not to laugh.

"I'm trying, believe me. Let's take a look at the next one shall we."

Katherine noticed the distance Todd was careful to maintain as they walked slowly to the next one. They both gazed at the painting. "Nope," Todd said after about a minute. "Still not getting it."

Katherine laughed. "You're impossible."

28

"I see someone is having a good time," Ashley said beaming at her friend. The minute she had seen them together the night of the banquet, Ashley had been convinced that Todd was the man that would drag her friend out her rut. She personally called Todd to invite him to the art show, carefully dropping the hint that Katherine would be there.

"I am trying to get Katherine to help me pick something out for my apartment. " Todd asked sounding serious. "She seems to like this one."

"It's really something isn't it?" Ashley's smile grew wider.

"That, it is," Todd winked at Katherine as he turned back to look at the painting thoughtfully.

Katherine bit her lip to keep from laughing.

"Let me know when you decide, "Ashley said as she moved to say hello to another art critic.

Katherine bursted out laughing. "You're going get us kicked out," she managed to make out.

"No *you're* going get us kicked out. You're the one who's laughing."

Katherine clamped her mouth shut, but not before a giggle escaped.

"That's it we're going outside. I'm not going to let us get kicked out on our butts."

Katherine nodded and started toward the door. She noticed the distance Todd kept between them. He seemed so different from the way he had been at the park. He hadn't attempted to touch her all evening.

"There," Todd said when they stepped out the door. "More dignified than getting kicked out isn't it?"

"Much," Katherine said with a chuckle. She couldn't remember the last time she had had this much fun. The man was simply adorable. And sexy, she thought as her eyes swept over him.

He was wearing a dark jacket over a white shirt, no tie. He had left the first two buttons of his shirt undone. She noticed that his wavy hard hair was still a little longer than convention. His blue eyes were warm and friendly as he regarded her. The look of male appreciation she had seen in them before were nowhere to be found.

Katherine wasn't sure why she felt disappointed but she did. She knew that the black knee length dress with the thin straps made the most of her curvy figure and was complemented by the high strappy shoes she was wearing. Her hair was down and her make up was immaculate. Everyone seemed to have noticed how nice she looked-everyone except Todd that is. She might as well have been wearing a sac.

"I see you're quite the art conossoir," she said drily.

"Actually, I love art," he said motioning her to join him as he started to walk slowly down the side walk.

"Could have fooled me."

Todd smiled. "I like art, but I am partial to the impressionists. Monet, Renoir, Van Gough...you know."

"Me too."

"You're not really into that whole abstract art, are you?"

Katherine hesitated. "No," she said finally.

Todd laughed. "Thought so."

"I don't hate it, I mean some are great-really powerful, but some of them are really complicated. "

"I guess, you just have to learn how to look at them and see what's beneath the surface. It takes a lot of patience. But then again, people are kind of like that too."

Katherine looked at him surprised both by his answer and his comparison. "I guess you're right," she said softly.

They walked a little further in companiable silence before Todd said, "I think it might be safe to go back in, what do think?"

"I think you're right," Katherine smiled up at him.

When they got to the gallery, Todd disappeared while she said hello to a new old friends. He later found her standing in the same painting she had been looking at when he first saw her.

"It was really great seeing you, Katherine," he said smiling down at her.

"You're leaving?" Katherine couldn't keep the disappointment from her voice.

"I have a case I'm working on."

"Oh."

"It was really good seeing you Katherine," he repeated. "I had a great time."

"So did I," Katherine said with a smile. He leaned toward her and Katherine half-expected him to kiss her on the cheek, but he straightened abruptly, smiled and was out the door. This time it was Katherine who was left with her jaw hanging. Maybe he wasn't interested in her anymore. But he'd been so attentive and friendly all evening. Maybe he just wanted them to be friends. Katherine looked at the painting frustrated. He was right about one thing though, she said to herself, people are definitely complicated.

Todd closed his eyes and took a deep breath when he collapsed into the back seat of the cab. It had taken all of his restraint to be with Katherine tonight. Standing so close to her without being able to touch her had been

30

frustrating. Especially in that dress. The dress hugged every curve in her body and showed off her shapely legs. Her creamy skin looked so soft his fingers were twitching to reach out and touch her. But it was her smiles and laughter that almost undid him. He had to brace himself every time her shoulder shook with laughter.

He smiled as he recalled how disappointed she sounded when he said he was leaving. It had taken all of his will power not stay and not to kiss her inviting lips. But he knew where that little kiss would lead and he wasn't entirely sure that Katherine was emotionally ready for that. Todd knew that she liked him despite how cool and aloof she acted, but what he needed was for her to trust him. He had a feeling that she wasn't the type of women who gave herself or her body freely. He didn't want to ruin his chances with her by rushing things with her.

As he stared out into the night, Todd wondered what had changed. Three days ago, all he was interested was his work and proving himself to the partners at the law firm. He certainly wasn't interested in getting emotionally entangled with anyone. No strings attached. Not until he was ready. That had been his M.O. but one look at Katherine and he'd done a 180.

He was actually the one making the effort. Usually the women made a play for him. Maybe this wasn't such a great idea. What about his goals? What was he thinking? This is the worst time for him to get into a relationship. His career was just about to take off. He can't afford any distractions. He had a case to win.

After making a suggestion that helped keep one of the firm's biggest clients, Mr. Goodman, out of court, his professional life seemed to have taken a turn. Mr. Goodman had insisted that Todd represent him. Todd knew that this didn't sit too well with the partners, but he was overjoyed. This was the break he'd been waiting for. This was exactly what he needed to finally make partner. He did not mind the extra hours it would mean. Making partner was all ever dreamed since college. Before he met Katherine, that is.

Chapter Five

Katherine stretched out leisurely as she tried to decide whether or not to go for her morning run. Part of her wanted to stay snuggled up under the blanket but another part of her longed to see the country. She was in Litchfield, a picturesque little town in Connecticut, away from the grime and grind of the city. Everything would be green, the country air fresh and the weather forecast promised that it would be a beautiful day.

Katherine glanced over at her bedside clock; it was 8:45. She still had enough time to go for morning run and be back in time for brunch. Bu then again, she was pretty comfortable. She snuggled deeper under the covers sighing. Out of nowhere, the image of Todd looking down at her with his knowing eyes popped into her head and she she began to wonder.... Knowing where those thoughts were likely to lead her, Katherine jerked out of bed and decided that yes, she really did want to go running!

She forced herself to concentrate on the beautiful scenery as she jogged, determined to not to let anything or *anyone* ruin her favorite day of the week. Well, her favorite and her least favorite. Katherine both loved and hated Sundays. She has had this love-hate relationship with Sundays for as long as she could remember.

She hated Sundays because that meant that the next day was Monday and the week-end is over. On the other hand, she loved Sunday because it represented her time to spend with loved ones. of the brunch her mother always organized. Every last Sunday of the month, Emily would organize a buffet big in their country house. It was strictly a family affair. Her parents, her brother Steven, uncle Bob, Aunt Margret and her. And sometimes Ashley. It started when Katherine was five and soon became a family tradition.

Her father often said that one of the smartest things he had ever made was letting his wife talk him into buying the property. Katherine agreed. Most of her fond childhood memories were in the house. Whether it was sliding down the banister or sneaking up to her brother's tree house. To Katherine, Litchfield was more of a home than the New York town house ever was.

The white colonial house with its high columns, country-style kitchen and large fire places stood on a 13 acres of land and had large windows that opened up to rolling hills and beautiful sunsets. Gazing at the house as she tried to catch her breath before going in, Katherine wished not for the first time that she could give her children the same happy childhood her parents gave her.

Usually, Katherine liked to take her time in the bathroom but today she showered and quickly slipped into a white summer dress and dashed downstairs. She couldn't wait for brunch to get started. Not because she was hungry but because she was dying of curiosity. Her mother had told her that her brother said that he would be bringing a friend.

He didn't say who, but Katherine had a feeling that it was a girl; the girl he had been seeing. He had been so secretive about the new girl he had been seeing. Katherine had a feeling it was because he was worried about what they would think. Steve hadn't brought a girl home since he was in college and even then, Katherine had a feeling she had sort of invited herself and Steven wasn't happy about it.

Although, Emily never said a word, Katherine knew that their mother would like nothing better than to see the apple of her eye settle down with someone. The fact that Steve was the favorite child never bothered Katherine. She reveled in the freedom it gave her. She wasn't put on a pedestal and didn't have to live up to any expectations.

Steven, on the other hand, was and had to. Her parents all but made him out to be a saint. Katherine almost felt sorry for the poor girl he had invited for lunch. Although her parents were liberal enough, she couldn't help but feel that they might expect too much and end up disappointed.

"Dear god, I hope she's not a model," she'd heard her mother say to Aunt Margaret and they both shook their heads. Most of the girls Steve dated were models, actresses or skinny debutantes that lived on carrots and yoghurt.

"Believe me, he would not bring a model here." Katherine said drily. She thought that most of the girls he dated were silly and that it was very unlikely that Steve would even consider settling down with them. He probably liked them because they were easy and expected so little from him.

This mystery-girl, whoever she was, had to be different. Katherine was sure of it. "I think we're all in for a surprise."

And she was right. Katherine's jaw almost fell to the ground when he walked in with none other than Nicole! Nicole was the person he'd been seeing, the person he wanted to introduce her to when the time is right! She could not believe it. Thinking about it, it was obvious. How could she have been so blind? Both Steve and Nicole had told her they were seeing someone new but they refused to tell her who. They seemed really cozy at the art show and Ashley said she thought she saw them leave together.

"You little sneak! You never told me that you and Steve were seeing each other!" Katherine exclaimed hugging her friend.

Nicole blushed.

"I saw you two together at Ashley's art gallery, but..." Katherine whipping her head from Steve to Nicole and back to Steve.

"Well, it's good to see to you," Steve said drily wrapping his sister in a bear hug. Katherine suspected was to shut her up.

"Why didn't you tell me?" she demanded, hands in hips.

"Oh and have you give us the same warm welcome you just did," Steve countered. "Where's everyone anyway?" he asked as he began to lead Nicole further into the house.

33

"Mom's upstairs and dad's in his study. Why don't you get Nicole a drink? I'll stay here and keep her company."

Steve looked like he was about to say something but changed his mind. "Don't let her bully you, okay," he said giving Nicole's hand a reassuring squeeze before heading to his favorite room in the house, the kitchen.

Katherine linked hands with her friend and pulled her into the sitting room. "You have to tell me everything. I can't believe you kept this from me!"

"I'm sorry Katey. I just didn't want to jinx it," Nicole said as they settled onto the sofa in the lavishly furnished sitting room.

Katherine nodded. "Must be serious. Steve's never brought anyone over for brunch."

"I know," Nicole answered. "I mean it is." Nicole smoothed her dress and then tucked her hair behind her ears something she did when she was nervous.

"Do you think your parents...?"

"Don't be silly! You know mom and dad love you. Besides, I'm sure they'll be so relieved that he didn't show up with some air-head model. "

They both laughed.

Nicole hesitated before reaching for her friend's hand. "Are you okay with it? I mean, with us?"

"Of course it is Nicole, I couldn't be happier!"

"Thanks that means a lot. I mean, you're one of my best friends." Nicole said squeezing Katherine's hand.

"So, are you going to give me the juicy details or am I going to have to drag it out of you?"

Nicole giggled. "Remember David?"

How could I forget? David was a good looking successful plastic surgeon Nicole had dated. Katherine was surprised the relationship had lasted as long as it did. The man was a first class jerk. He made Greg look like a saint. Katherine had been happy to see the relationship end. David had a way of making Nicole feel like dirt. "Oh you mean the guy who has a picture of himself on his bedside table?"

"Yes, that asshole."

A wide-eyed Katherine gapped at her friend. In the twenty years she'd known Nicole, she had never heard her use such strong language. "Alright, who are you and what did you do to friend?"

Nicole chuckled. "But he is."

34

"Well, I'm glad we're finally on the same page. What about him?"

"Well, he and Steven have quite a few friends in common which meant that he and I bumped into Steven quite a lot. The minute I stopped paying attention to Steven, he started paying attention to me. About two months ago we bumped into each other again at a doctor's benefit and David was being ... well, David. I needed a shoulder to cry on and Steve offered me his and... "

"If you're done interrogating my girlfriend, we'd all like to eat now," Steve called out from the dining room.

Brunch was perfect. Emily and Margret had outdone themselves, as usual. Extra effort had gone into today's brunch because of the possible new addition to the family. Even though Nicole was shy and clearly nervous, she fit right in with the rest of the family. As the meal came to an end, Katherine smiled at across table at Nicole and her brother Steve. She was thrilled to see them so deeply in love.

She was glad that her brother had stopped playing the field long enough to notice the pretty brunette. Katherine watched he brother cover Nicole's hand with his. That was when she realized that she was the only single person at the table. She was surprised at the loneliness that washed through as she witness the exchange. Maybe dating wouldn't be such a bad idea, she said to herself thinking of how much fun she had with Todd at the gallery.

"So how did things go with mystery-guy?" Nicole asked in a teasing voice.

"What do you mean?"

"I saw you two at the gallery."

Katherine blushed. "It's nothing serious. It's not what you think at all. We just met." She cringed. Even to her own ears she sounded flustered. She stole a glance at her parents and was relieved to see that they were engrossed in what Uncle Paul was saying.

Steve and Nicole exchanged a look. "But you like him." Steve said slowly. Katherine averted her gaze, taking a sip of water. She never could keep anything from her brother.

Her brother laughed. "Well, it's nice to see that you're not pining over that asshole anymore."

"I never said I liked him." She could feel cheeks going warm.

"You didn't have to," he answered with a smile. Katherine was glad when her brother excused himself to answer his phone.

"Do you still have feelings for Greg?" Nicole asked in a concerned voice.

Katherine sighed. She wished she could say that she didn't. "I'm not sure," she answered honestly.

"You might wanna consider giving mystery guy a chance," Nicole suggested. "What's he like anyway?"

"Persistent," Katherine said and they both laughed. She was glad when her brother returned and the conversation took another turn.

Katherine returned to the city that night feeling perplexed. The problem with Todd wasn't that she didn't like him. It was that she liked him too much. That fact that she was so attracted to him didn't help matters either. Maybe it was a good thing that he hadn't called her all week. She didn't want to get involved with anyone. She wasn't a masochist. She was not about to put herself in the line of fire. Again!

Todd woke up looking forward to his morning run, more so than usual. He loved running. He loved the feel of the wind against his face and sound of his feet pounding against the tarmac. He also loved the exhilarating feeling of freedom that running gave him. Running had always been a part of his life. He had been on the track team both in high school and college.

He'd been so busy in Chicago, he hadn't had a chance to squeeze in a work out or go running. Not wanting to keep Josh waiting for him, Todd jumped out of bed and into his clothes and sprinted from his apartment all the way to the park. He smiled as he watched his friend chatting animatedly as he stretched out next to a blond. Of course Josh would pick up women even when he went jogging- the man was a dog.

As he approached them, he realized that there was something familiar about the way the woman moved; there was an elegance about her. The blond turned slightly lifting her face to the sun with her eyes closed. Todd froze when he realized who it was. I guess the day is off to a good start, he thought. Even in her black track bottoms and gray tank top, her hair pulled up in a high pony tail without a stitch of make up, she looked hot. Although it'd been over a week since he'd last seen, the attraction he felt towards her hadn't abated one bit.

"Hey," he said slightly out of breath. "I'm gone less than a week and you replace me."

"What can I say? She's cute," Josh replied smiling.

"You're right, she is cute" Todd said locking eyes with Katherine. Katherine felt herself blush.

"Well, when you two done are flirting you can catch up with me," Katherine said and took off trying not to feel self-conscious. She could feel Todd's eyes on her as they scrambled to catch up with her.

Katherine tried to concentrate on the lyrics of the songs she was listening to but every cell in her body was aware of the fact that Todd was right next to her. It didn't help that his t-shirt did very little to hide his strong biceps and rippling abdominal muscles. Katherine was more wired up at the end of their 5 mile run than she was at the beginning. Being next to him gave her an adrenalin rush, she felt like she could run another 5 miles. She shifted her weight from one foot to the other as Josh and Todd began to stretch out. She knew that she would have a hard time keeping her eyes off him, especially with the sheen of sweat coating his skin.

"Same time, tomorrow?" she said to Josh avoiding looking at Todd.

"Sure," Josh said as he started to so his stretches.

She nodded and started off. "Hey, aren't you going to stretch out?" Josh called after her.

"I will when I get home."

Todd watched in confusion as she broke into a jog. Was she running away? First she acts like he doesn't exist; now she takes off without so much as a good bye? "Did I say something?"

"Huh?"

"I mean Katherine…"

Josh chuckled and patted his friend on the back shaking his head apologetically. "Todd, my friend, you have a lot to learn about women."

Took gave him a blank stare.

"She likes you, man," Josh said somewhat exasperated.

"Really?" he asked as he glanced at her retreating figure. He "You think so?"

"Look, I have known Katherine my entire life and there is definitely something there."

"Oh." Todd thought about how disappointed she looked when he said he was leaving the art show early, he recalled how she always seemed to hold her breath every time he came close to her or how she tried to avoid looking him in the eye and when she did, she seemed to have as much difficulty as he did tearing her gaze away. Todd couldn't help the goofy smile the spread across his face. She liked him. She wasn't just attracted to him; she might actually feel something for him. The possibility made him feel as high as a kite. "You know what? I think you are right," he said slowly.

"What are you doing here? Go after her!" Josh urged. "But if you hurt her I'll kill you."

Katherine felt like a coward for running away, but she didn't know what else to do. Todd was the last person she expected to see that morning and the effect that had on her was so strong it scared her. She didn't like not being in control of her feelings and emotions. When she was around him, she turned into a bundle of nerves.

The fact that she was all sweaty and probably looked like a hot mess this morning did not help matters. She hadn't so much as glanced at the mirror before leaving the house. She groaned when she saw him jogging next to her. She couldn't believe that he had actually followed her! She ignored him for a few seconds before caving

37

in. "You know in some states, that would be considered stalking." She said slowing down slightly.

"Well, in a lot of states, *that* would be considered running away."

That brought her to a stop. "I'm not running away," she argued hands on her hips, lifting her chin stubbornly.

"Right. So what was that all about?" he challenging also placing his hands on his hips.

"What are you talking about?" she said innocently, looking away from his penetrating gaze.

"Where were you trying so hard to ignore me back there?"

"I wasn't."

"Oh really?"

"Yes, I just happen not to be a morning person."

"You're lying," he taunted.

"I am not lying," she said angrily blood rushing to her cheeks, her hands balling up into fists at her side.

"You are," he went on confidently. "In fact, I think you're afraid to be alone with me."

Katherine had to hold herself back from punching that cocky grin off his face. Why did he have to be so exasperating? "That's ridiculous! I'm not afraid of being a lone with you," she practically shouted. She felt like stamping her feet when she saw his smile grow wider.

"Fine, prove it."

She tried to convince herself that the reason she suddenly felt out of breath was because she'd been running. It had nothing to do with the way he was looking at her. "What do you mean?" she asked working to keep her voice steady.

"Have dinner with me," he said softly. She glared at him. "Fine, coffee-even you can't say no to that. Unless…"he let his word trail off.

Katherine bit her lower lip. Coffee couldn't hurt. Besides, she didn't want him thinking that she was afraid of being alone with him.

"I'll pick you up at four."

She fumed. The man had some nerve. She hadn't even said yes. First he leaves town and doesn't even bother to call and then he assumes that she would drop everything and have coffee with him just because he asked. So what if he was cute?! He was probably used to women falling at his feet. Well, she certainly wasn't one of

38

them!

Before she launched into her tirade, Todd leaned forward and silenced her with his lips. His lips felt so warm and soft as they moved slowly over hers. Her anger dissolved and the tension left her jaw. Despite of all the warning bells going off in her head, she closed her eyes and parted her lips, hands dropping to her side.

"You smell so good," he murmured against her lips as he inhaled her sweet fragrance-she smelt like vanilla, baby powder and freesia. Todd found the combination intoxicating. His fingers itched to feel the smoothness of her skin, but he kept his hands at his side. They were in a public place and he was trying his best to keep the kiss PG.

"I'm all sweaty," she murmured back, her head spinning at the sensations flowing through her.

He moved his lips to her ear, "I think I like you all sweaty." Katherine shivered. "Say yes. Please." His warm breath fanned her face as he pressed his forehead on hers, his finger tips caressing her cheeks.

Unable to find her voice, Katherine nodded. He cupped her face depositing a chaste kiss on her lips. Katherine opened her eyes to see his retreating figure. A strong part of her was giddy with excitement. Another part of her wanted to scream, to scream and shout at her own weakness. She couldn't believe how it easy it had been for him to coax her out of her decision to stay away from him. She would have said yes to anything he asked her and the most annoying thing about it was that he knew it.

Katherine turned around and headed to her apartment before doing anything stupid. She took the stairs rather than the elevator not stopping till she was in the safety of her apartment with the door bolted behind her. She slumped against the door panting. Sliding to the floor, Katherine dropped her head in her hands, clearly things were not going the way she planned. Katherine didn't know how long she sat there.

By the time she got up, she was sore. She stretched out before heading to the shower. The hot shower helped relax a little, but she was still a little wound up. Only one thing can do the trick. She headed to the kitchen and started pulling out pots and pans. That seemed to do the trick , before long she was calm as she hummed and baked.

Chapter Six

Todd's heart raced in his chest as he waited for Katherine to open the door. He hadn't meant to come by so soon. Hell, he hadn't meant to come by at all. That was not part of the plan. He had been trying hard to block her out of his thoughts all week. He had buried himself in his work. He told himself that the best thing to do was to avoid her. The girl scared the hell out of him. He knew that there was no way he could keep things light between them.

Asking her out wasn't a good idea and now here he was pounding on her door. Another bad idea. He couldn't help it. He didn't want to wait till tonight to see her. He didn't think he would survive that long. The kiss in the park had left him shaken. He hadn't meant to kiss her. He didn't know what had gotten into him. But there was no going back now.

He knew that he what he felt for Katherine went way beyond attraction. Although he wasn't ready to acknowledge exactly what that feeling was, he knew that he couldn't stay away even if he did try.

His heart leaped in his chest when she finally opened the door. She was wearing white city shorts and a dark blue tank, her hair pulled back in a high pony tail with loose tendrils framing her face. Her expression went from impatience to mild surprise. "You're early, you know," she said placing one hand on her hip and arching her eye brows.

Todd chuckled nervously. Maybe this wasn't such a great idea. It looked like she was busy. He thought about making his excuses and returning later, but his curiosity got the better of him when he noticed the kitchen mitt she was holding. "I thought you might need a hand."

Katherine folded her arms across her chest. "You thought I might need a hand?"

Todd shrugged.

"It's only 2 o'clock, you know."

Todd ignored the not-so-subtle hint. It was obvious she wanted him gone, but Todd had no intention of leaving. He was having too much fun agitating her. "I think you've already established that I'm early," he said.

"Quit trying to be clever, counselor. It's not cute," Katherine snapped.

"I wasn't trying, but thanks for noticing." He asked peering over her shoulder into the apartment. "What *are* you doing anyway?"

"None of your business."

"Aren't you going to ask me in?"

40

"You're not going to go away, are you?"

"Probably not."

Katherine hesitate, glanced at him and then back into the apartment and then sighed throwing her hands up in an impatient gesture. "Fine. Come in," she said with an exaggerated sweeping gesture.

Mouth-watering aroma hit Todd the minute he walked in. "What is that smell?"

"I was cooking and thanks to you, it's probably burning!" ," Katherine said in a somewhat strained voice as she walked stiffly past him to the kitchen area.

Todd followed her looking around the apartment. It was a beautiful apartment with huge windows overlooking the park. The décor was exquisite. It was homey with comfortable sofas with throws draped over them and lots of pillows. There were also a few antique pieces scattered around.

She sure wasn't kidding when she said she was cooking. There were bowls and pans and flour littered the kitchen. "Sure smells good in here. Anything I can do to help?" The smile she gave him was full of mischief making wonder if he was going to regret his offer.

"Well, you could help me clean up," she said innocently pointing at the large pile dirty dishes. She grabbed a pair of yellow rubber gloves and shoved them at him.

You're not getting rid of me that easily. He donned on the gloves and got to work . They worked in silence for a while, Erica Badou playing in the background. Todd watched her as he dried the dishes. He had never seen her this at ease. She seemed so content padding around the kitchen bare feet cooking up a storm. "You do this often?" he asked breaking the silence.

"No, not as much as I used," she said as she pulled something out the oven. "Now I just do it to clear my head."

Interesting. "Kinda like therapy," he said as he settled on to a stool at the counter.

"Yeah," she responded sounding preoccupied.

"What's been on your mind lately?" he asked careful to keep the curiosity from his voice.

"Nothing really," she answered quickly turned to shut the oven, but not before Todd noticed that she was blushing furiously.

"You are trying to clear your mind of nothing," Todd retorted drily.

"Not thing. I mean, nothing important."

"Oh?"

41

"If you really must know, I'm worried about the party I'm putting together for Ashley."

"Aha." Todd smiled. The woman was such a terrible liar. "And you…"

"… If you would quit being a nosy lawyer for five seconds, I'd like you to taste something." She lifted the foil off the pan she had brought out of the oven and a delicious aroma filled the kitchen. She dug a fork into the quiche, brought it to her lips and blew on it several times. "Here, try this," she said and lifted the fork to his lips.

"Mmm! This is amazing. Where did you learn to cook like that?"

"I spent a lot of time with my aunt Margaret when I was growing up."

"You learnt all this from your aunt?" he asked pointing at the casseroles and pies on the counter.

Katherine laughed. "I picked a few things in Paris, but this, this I learnt from Aunt Margaret," she picked up a spoon, opened a pot and stirred it and brought the spoon to her mouth blowing it. "Try this." She lifted the spoon to his lips.

"Wow! This is really good."

She smiled. She picked up a fork and dug into one of the pies, "Here try this," she said lifting the fork to his lips. He did a thumbs up sign as he chewed, enjoying the intimacy of the moment. "You want me ti fix you a plate?"

"Oh yeah," he answered with a laugh. As he watched her as she piled two plates with a variety of the things she had made he felt a longing he couldn't quite identify.

"Here, why don't you take these to the living room. I'll get the wine."

"And water," he said.

"And water," she repeated with a smile.

A few minutes later, they settled on her couch eating in companionable silence.

"Do you play?" Todd asked pointing at the expensive grand piano sitting in the far corner.

She laughed shaking her head. "Not very well. I'm afraid I'm a little tone deaf."

"Looks good though. Adds character to the place. You've done the place up nicely."

Katherine sipped her wine. "I had a great a decorator."

Todd's gaze swept the room once more. "The place has you written all over it. Classy, homey and very adventurous."

Katherine let out a surprise laugh. She had decorated the place herself to fit her taste and personality. "You seem to know so much about me and I don't know a thing about you," she shifting the attention away from her.

"What do you want to know?"

"I don't know... um... where did you grow up?"

"California."

"Does your family still live there?"

"I'm an only child and my parents died when I was young."

"Oh my god, I'm so sorry," she put her plate down and inched closer to him. "I didn't mean to bring up any bad memories."

"It's okay. It was long time ago," Todd said with a shrug. Todd found himself telling Katherine how he lost his parents in a car accident when he was ten years old. Both his parents had lost their parents shortly after Todd was born. His mother had been an only child so Todd was assigned to the custody to his only living relative-his father's younger sister, aunt Celeste .

Though Todd had only met her a few times before his parents passed away, he could sense that she and his mother disliked each other intensely. Aunt Celeste initially complained about having to "waste her youth rearing Tom's boy"and even suggested that Todd be given up for adoption till she found out that her estranged brother had left a sizeable fortune. She quickly went through his parents' money with her trips to Europe and extravagant lifestyle.

When she realized that the funds were running low, she threatened to pull Todd out of the expensive private school he went to and enroll him in a public school. Unable to get her hands on his trust fund, she had kicked him out of the house the minute he'd turned eighteen.

Todd hadn't minded when she sold the house when he graduated from high school. He wanted to be as far away from her as he could so he applied to colleges on the east coast. He paid his college tuition and with the help of his father's friend, wisely invested the rest of the funds in various internet companies.

"Where's your aunt now?" Katherine asked. She couldn't imagine how miserable Todd's childhood must have been.

"Last I heard, she married some movie director and moved to Australia. I haven't seen her in almost ten years."

"Ten years!"

"Yeah. Can't say that I miss her though," Todd said with a dry laugh.

43

Katherine bit her lip. I sure put my foot in it this time, she thought.

"As you can imagine," Todd went on, "college was way more fun."

"Yeah, Josh told me about all about your wild days at college," Katherine quipped glad that he had made light of the matter.

"Well, don't believe everything you hear," Todd said shifting in his seat. He didn't want Katherine to think that he was anything like Josh. Josh didn't believe in relationships and considered sex a sport. He was best known for throwing the wildest parties and for being a player. Todd had stuck to his books determined to make something of himself and to his girlfriend Madeleine-that was, till he found her in bed with someone else.

In his anger, Todd had gone on a sex spree hooking up with almost as many girls as josh. It wasn't something he was proud of. He hoped that josh hadn't included that bit in his accounts to Katherine. "Why Europe, for college I mean?" he asked half because he was curious but mostly to deflect the attention on him.

"I guess I wanted to go some place different," she said pouring herself more wine. "I always liked Europe and I wanted to learn French so I went to college in Switzerland and then moved to France afterwards."

"Must have been quite an experience,"

"Oh, it was. I love Paris," she said with a smile.

"And what made you come home after so long?"

"Greg," she answered simply. She didn't know how much Josh had told him about her ex, but since he had opened up to her about his family, she decided she might as well tell him. "We met three years ago. He was a big client on mine, always calling to have flowers delivered. That should have tipped me off right there. Anyway, he came by the shop one day to buy flowers. He was so refined and charming-very different from anyone I had ever met. I guess I was fascinated by him. He took me out to lunch and before you know it we had practically moved in together."

"What happened?" Todd managed to ask through his haze of jealousy.

She bit her lower lip,slowly setting don her drink on the coffee table. "He got transferred to Dubai and I thought he would ask me to go with him, but he didn't," she said with a slight shrug.

"Greg is an idiot! "

"I know," Katherine said with a smile. "He was also my first love."

"I wouldn't put much stock in first love. My first love cheated on me with the president of the chess club."

"Really?"

"Yes. He was about yey high, he wore suspenders and his glasses were about six inches thick."

Katherine busted out laughing. "Your first love cheated on you with Steve Urkle?!"

Todd laughed. "As you can imagine it was quite a blow to my ego. It took me a while to get over that."

"And I thought I had it bad," she muttered laughing with him. "I told you mine, now you tell me yours. What's your story-post college?"

"Not much to tell really. The last serious relationship I was in lasted about a year. She left me for a stock broker."

"Oh I am sorry to hear that," Katherine asked.

"Oh, it's okay. It was two years ago," he said with a slight shrug.

So he had been hurt before. She wandered if he had been in love with the girl; if he still was. She wondered why she cared. "Do you still love her?" Katherine regretted the words as soon as they were out of her mouth. She could feel her face going up in flames.

"At the time I thought I did," he said slowly. "But it was never going to work out anyway." he shrugged again. "Things weren't right from the beginning. The signs were all there. But when you put so much of yourself out there you just don't want to accept defeat so you turn a blind eye and sweep things under the rug till it finally blows up in your faee, you know."

"I know, " Katherine agreed. Their eyes met and held briefly. "Are you done?" she asked as she reached for his plate.

Todd shot to his feet. "I'm doing the dishes today, remember," he said taking the plates and heading to the kitchen.

Katherine picked up their glasses and followed him to the kitchen. She settled on the kitchen stools and watched him load up the dish washer. She'd forgotten how good it felt to cook for someone. Cooking and baking had always relaxed her.

She had been annoyed when he showed up at her doorstep thinking there was no way she would be able to relax with him anywhere near. She had been wrong. She actually enjoyed having him over. He was easy to talk to and he made her laugh.

What a day this was turning out to be, she thought as she pulled out the scrunchie holding her hair up and proceeded to comb the tresses of her hair with her fingers.

"Greg's an idiot," Todd repeated softly. Her eyes flew open to see him leaning against the sink, his eyes burning

45

intently. Katherine's breath hitched in her throat. She let her arms fall to rest on the counter. And just like that, the look was gone leaving her to wonder if it she had imagined it. There was no way she could have imagined that-not with the way herself was still responding to it.

He approached her in his easy manner but his eyes looked guarded. As he reached for her hand pulling her off the stool, Katherine held her breath thinking that he was going to kiss her. He didn't. He tugged her hand pulling her behind him as he made his way to the door. She realized with a pang of disappointment that he was leaving. He hesitated at the door, his expression wistful like he was battling whether or not to leave.

"Greg is an idiot," he said repeated softly brushing the length of her cheekbones with his fingertips, his expression so intense it startled her. And then he was gone.

Katherine closed the door slowly and walked to the living room window in a daze. Her face still felt warm from his touch. It was as though his fingers had left a trail on fire on her cheeks. She watched him from her window as he looked up at her apartment before disappearing into a cab. She stood there for a long time trying to sort out her feelings. She had felt this connected to anyone. Not even with Greg.

I guess the old adage is true-the fastest way to get over a guy is to get a new one. The more time she spent with Todd the less she thought about Greg. She could feel the gaping hole Greg had left in her heart slowly begin to fill up again and for the first time in a long time she felt almost whole again. Almost.

Katherine went back to kitchen where she wrapped the food and put them in the refrigerator and then return to the living room and curled up with a book. She was deeply engrossed in the story and the beeping sound of her phone startled her. Even as she chided herself for letting him get too close too fast, she couldn't help the smile that formed at her lips as she read the text message on her phone. *Pick you up at 7, wear something comfortable. T.*

Chapter Seven

After spending the whole afternoon with Katherine, Todd's apartment felt so cold and empty. He didn't have any paper work to go over and he couldn't imagine spending the evening alone with Chinese take out and cable TV.

He loved seeing her in her kitchen. She looked even sexier bare feet in her tiny shorts humming as she worked. It was almost too painful to watch. He found the fact that she was such a great cook fascinating. He didn't know anyone their age who could cook like that. He doubted that any of her socialite friends knew how to boil an egg.

He wondered whether she would still be up for their date tonight. As he contemplated where to take her, he remembered the tickets Josh had given the day before. They were front row tickets to a basketball game. He wasn't sure whether she even liked basketball. It wouldn't surprise him if she did. The girl was full of surprises.

I hope she wouldn't think I'm pushy, he thought. He didn't want to rush her and if he were honest with himself, he didn't want to rush himself either. His resolve not to get into a serious relationship seemed to flown out the window. He simply couldn't to stay away from her. The more he saw her, the more he wanted to see her. Her presence was addicting and the connection he felt with her was so strong, it scared him.

He knew without a doubt that she was the kind of person he could see himself falling in love with. He loved everything about her. He loved her sense of humor, her wit, her ability to surprise him, not to mention the way she looked. She had the most beautiful smile and eyes he could drown in for days. And of course, there was her figure.

She seemed so comfortable in her own skin and exuded the same confidence in tracks with her gorgeous hair pulled away form her face without a stitch of make up as she did fully made up in an haute couture dinner gown designed to make the most out of her already flawless figure.

He smiled when he remembered the disappointment in her eyes when she realized that it was leaving. It was the second time she had given him that look and it left him riding on a jittery high. Despite her cool demeanor, she really did enjoy being around him. He dropped into the sofa and punched her number then disconnected it before it rang. He would send her a text instead. He didn't want her thinking that he was obsessed or anything. A few seconds later, his phone vibrated and he smiled.

When Todd picked her up that night, she was wearing tan capris, a black cotton wrap-around shirt and espadrilles. She had a Louis Vuitton monogram purse slung over her shoulder. She looked almost shy as she answered the door bell. Todd couldn't stop his gaze from traveling slowly over her. The cotton shirt clung to her like second skin. The tan pants which just covered her knees paired with high shoes drew his eye to her slim shapely legs. Her hair was pulled back in a low ponytail at the nape of her neck and she didn't seem to be wearing much make up. She looked amazing. Todd smile shaking his head slightly to convince himself this was real.

"You said comfortable, this *is* comfortable," she said defensively.

"You look great."

She rolled her eyes as she turned around to lock the door. The expression was so unexpected from her normal behavior, Todd had to smile.

"Where are we going anyway?" she asked as they made their way to the elevator.

"I thought we could go to a basketball game and then the park."

"And this, I suppose is not the appropriate attire for a basketball game," she said sarcastically.

"No, you look great. Really. I just thought that you might be uncomfortable walking in those," he answered pointing to her high shoes.

"I'll be fine," she said a little embarrassed at how insecure she must have sounded. She had tried on seven different outfits before finally settling on this one. Maybe she should have stuck with jeans. She didn't know why she was nervous. She had spent the entire day with him after all. So what if this was their first official date? I am just going to relax and have a good time, she told herself sneaking a glance at him.

Todd looked yumm, as Ashley would say. Dressed in a gray Ralph Lauren polo shirt that showed off his broad shoulders and dark blue jeans, he looked more like an actor than a lawyer. And try not to get caught staring, of course, she chided herself.

Katherine enjoyed the basketball game more than she thought she would. She wasn't a fan of basket ball, but it didn't take her long to get into the spirit.

"Hey, are you rooting for the enemy?"he asked with mock horror when she cheered.

"No, I'm rooting for my team."

"Since when did you have a team?"

"Since now."

"But I thought you didn't watch basketball."

"I don't."

"If you don't watch basketball, how is it that you have a team?"

49

"I like their jersey."

Todd hooted with laughter. "So you're supporting the enemy because you like their little blue outfits?"

"Well that and the fact that I think that they are going totally going to kick your team's butt."

"You do, do you?"

"Yup," she replied eyes full of laughter.

."Don't let the scores fool you, we're just getting started."

"Famous last words." As if on cue the team she was cheering for scored another basket. She cheered some more and then turned to face him giving him an I-told-you-so look.

"That's just luck."

"Ha!"

"You willing to put your money where your mouth is?

"Huh?"

"I mean, would you like to bet on it?" he said in his best imitation of the upper-east sider accent.

"I'm game. Bring it on," she challenged in her best imitation of the Brooklyn accent, something she picked up from one of her employees.

Todd chuckled. She sure was full of surprises. "Okay, you're on!"

"What are the stakes?"Katherine asked.

"Okay, let's see." Drumming his fingers against his thighs he considered how he could make things work for him. It was obvious that his team was likely to lose tonight. Any other night, being the die-hard fan he was, he would have been furious, but not tonight. Tonight he was having way too much fun. "Alright. Here it is," he said rubbing his hands together. "Your team wins, you get a kiss. My team wins I let you buy me dinner."

"You call that fair?"

"No, I call that a win-win situation," he said with mischievous grin.

"But…"

He placed a finger on her lips. "Shush, we're missing the game," he said.

The rest of the game passed by in blur. After the game, they walked around the park exchanging light banter and

50

funny stories. All through the laughter and chit chat, electricity seemed to buzz around them. Anticipation filled the air. She had been sure that he would after the game; it looked like he was about to before he spotted a colleague and went over to say hello. She was shocked when she glanced at her watch and realized that it was past eleven.

They made their way slowly back to her apartment. Katherine's hand shook slightly with as she unlocked her front door. *This is it. This is it*, she kept saying to herself. She had been sure he would kiss her in the park, but he didn't. Maybe he was just biding his time. This was the moment they had both been waiting for. No distractions, just the two of them.

He was standing so close to her, she could smell his cologne. *Should I ask him in for coffee? Would he think I'm easy if I did?* Katherine turned around slowly, bracing herself as she waited for him to claim his winnings. She stiffened and held her breath as his lips slowly descended towards hers, but instead of landing on her lips, the kiss landed on her forehead.

"Good night Katherine." he said with a strained smile before turning to walk away. Katherine stared after him long after he had vanished into the elevator. Feeling more than a little embarrassed, she walked into her apartment slowly and flung herself on her bed.

What the hell is going on? It had been the perfect date. He called that a kiss? Why was he playing hot and cold? It was obvious he liked her and it was obvious that he wanted to kiss her. There was no mistaking the look in his eyes. But why didn't he? Was he playing hard to get? What the hell was wrong with him? She lay there for a long time frustrated. She wasn't sure who she was angrier at-Todd for not kiss her properly or herself wanting him to.

Todd walked back to his apartment slowly. Watching her cheer, and yell and come alive at the basketball game had been more fun for him than actually watching the game. During the course of the evening, Todd noticed that the physical attraction he felt towards her had taken a back seat to the pull of her personality. Being with her was so easy it felt as though they'd known each other all their lives.

The more time they spent together, the more realized that what they had was more than just physical attraction. He knew that he wouldn't be able to stay away from her. He didn't want to even try. He desperately wanted her to trust him to see him as someone she could have a lasting relationship with. The only way to do that would be to repress their physical attraction and get to know one another. That was easier said than done. Even as they joked and exchanged light banter, it was there humming around them. The pull was so strong he didn't know how much longer he would be able to hold off.

It took more self-control than he knew he possessed to walk away. He was dying to kiss her, but he knew where that kiss would lead-they both did and he wasn't entirely sure she was ready for that. He saw the hesitation in her eyes as he leaned toward her to kiss. Maybe she wasn't over that guy. She did say that he was the love of her life and the decision to split up wasn't exactly mutual.

If Greg were to pick up the phone and call her, beg her forgiveness, would she run back to him? Todd wanted things to be good between them, he didn't want her to have any regrets. And he certainly did not want to get burned.

Ever since the night of the basket ball, Katherine relationship with Todd fell into a steady routine. Todd called her up every night and would either show up at her doorstep with coffee and the city's best bagels in the morning or would rush to the park to meet her for lunch. On week-ends, they went running and hung out together. And through it all, Todd kept his hands to himself.

"What about Greg?" he asked her one morning after their run. The question stunned Katherine into silence. His eyes bored into hers searching for answers.

"What *about* Greg?" she repeated raising one eyebrow.

He didn't answer, he merely shrugged and started doing his stretches. Katherine knew what he had been trying to ask. He wanted to know whether she was over Greg or not. The truth was, she never thought that she would ever get over him; till she met Todd, that is. All of a sudden, her relationship with Greg seemed so distant and lacking in substance.

She no longer missed him. She didn't miss cooking for him, she didn't miss their trips, the fancy dinner parties they threw, the lazy weekends they spent walking along the Seine River and she certainly did not miss picking up his dry-cleaning!

Todd had walked into her life and filled it so completely that she didn't even have room to think about Greg much less miss him. She felt as though she'd just landed in oz and all of a sudden, everything was in Technicolor. But she didn't tell him that. How could she tell him what he needed to hear without giving away too much?

His words on the park at the night of the basket ball game kept echoing in her head. "I'm a man who knows what he wants," he had said as they walked back to her apartment, "and I'm patient enough to wait for as long as it would take get it"'. The way he looked at when he said it made it clear to her that even though he had been telling her about his job, he wasn't only referring to work. He was talking about her.

Exhausted with trying to analyze her feelings and the guess at his, Katherine decided to just go with the flow let the chips fall where they may. Burying herself in tasks before her did little to keep her from thinking about him, or missing him. With a sinking sensation, she realized that she was already in free fall. She was falling in love with him and there was nothing she could do to stop it.

"Greg is not a part of my life anymore," she said after long silence. "You are."

Todd studied her face for a while before pull her into his arms and burying his face in her hair.

The week that followed was so busy for Todd; representing Goodman was not without its down side. The man always seemed to be at odds with law. Todd was completely swamped. His one day business trip to Chicago to meet with Goodman ended up being a three-day business trip-much to Todd's chagrin.

Katherine had become such a major part of his life; he had no idea what to do with himself when he wasn't with her. Talking to her on the phone every night seemed to make him miss her even more. By Friday, he was twitching to see her. He couldn't wait to get back to New York. He knew that she had had a trying week. Finding the right venue in New York for her friend's party had been a disaster. Everywhere was either fully book or not what Ashley had in mind.

Finally, Katherine had decided to have it at her family's house in the Hamptons. Then there were the invites to contend with. The guest list kept increasing that the "the intimate get-to-together" they had in mind threatened to turn into a convention. Everyone wanted in.

Everyone but Todd. Todd was so exhausted from his trip to Chicago and would have liked nothing better than to go back to his apartment after work and crash, but he had to see her, even if it was for a couple of hours. He would leave immediately after work and come back early in the morning for the brunch meeting with one of his partners. He would probably enjoy the drive. Being a New Yorker, driving wasn't a luxury he enjoyed very often.

By the time Todd got to the Hamptons, the party was in full swing. He looked around him in surprise. He hadn't expected to see so many people. So much for "small and intimate", he thought as h he followed the candles dotting the foot path to the back of the beach house. The cabana had been converted to a dance and floor but there people dancing around the pool, on the back porch and in the living room as well.

He squeezed through the throng of people occasionally stopping to ask where the birthday girl was. He pulled his cell phone out to call Katherine, hoping that she had her phone with her and would be able to hear it ringing over the craziness around when he spotted Ashley in a brilliant blue short strap-less dress that made her legs go for days. Relieved, he quickly made his way over. "Happy Birthday," he said kissing her on the cheek. "Great party."

Ashley beamed," Thanks. Katherine did a great job."

"Hey, I see you've managed to tear yourself from the boardroom. Good to see ya!" Josh slapped him on the back. "Thought you had an early meeting tomorrow?"

"I do."

Josh shot him a knowing smile, but didn't say anything. "You better get over there before Nathan pulls a fast one on you," he said nodding his head in their direction.

Todd was consumed with rage as he saw sandy-haired Nathan leering down at Katherine. He smiled slightly when he noticed her pull away as the Nathan tried to grab hold of her elbow. "I told you, I'm seeing someone," he heard her say as he approached them.

"Hey, babe," Todd said in her ear sliding his arm around her waist. She looked up at him in surprise. He leaned down to kiss her on the cheek but she turned slightly and the kiss landed on the corner of her lip. The greeting seemed so natural, as though they had been a couple for a long time. Resting his hand her hip, he extended his other hand at Nathan. "Hey Nathan, thanks for keeping an eye on my girl for me."

Nathan reddened. "No problem."

Ignoring him, Todd leaned over, caressed Katherine's cheek with the tips of his thumb, and covered her soft lips with his own. She sighed parting her lips as her heart continued to hammer in her chest. The kiss lasted barely more than a second, but it brought back all the yearning and longing crashing down on her that her knees almost buckled under her.

He heard Nathan mumble something and walked away. Katherine and Todd continued to gaze at each other, dazed at the effect such an innocent kiss had on them. "I missed you," he said softly.

Katherine smiled. "I missed you too," she admitted.

"You look great," he said and she did. She was wearing an emerald green halter neck dress with matching stilettos. He reached for the claw holding her hair up. "There, perfect," he said as her hair went cascading around her shoulder.

Katherine was surprised at how natural it felt to be in his arms. It was as though she belonged there, like they belonged together.

"No wonder the streets of Manhattan looked empty today-everyone is here," Todd said looking around when someone bumped into them.

"It seems that way doesn't it. I thought you said you had a meeting tomorrow morning?"

"I do, but I had to see you."

Katherine smiled up at him as they stood there locked in each other's gaze and embrace.

"Do you want to go outside?" she asked when someone else bumped into them again.

Todd nodded. Katherine led him to the patio overlooking the beach and they settled into a wicker chair. He put his arms around her pulling her close and she snuggled closer, resting her head against his chest. Todd sighed. Being with her was like finally coming home. All of a sudden the truth he had been trying to avoid for the past week became glaringly obvious. He had fallen in love with Katherine.

There was not question about it. He loved her with every once of his being. He loved her smile, he loved her laugh, he loved the little frown she did when she was concentrating, he loved the way she went from sounding very much an upper-east sider to sounding like she'd just stepped out of the Bronx. He loved her honesty and her ability to empathize with others. He loved her sense of humor and her wit.

He couldn't remember ever having this much fun with a woman, even arguing with her was fun. She was the one he wanted to wake up next to, to laugh with, to make a family with.

A part of him reminded him that he wasn't ready for that level of commitment yet. But it was a very small part.

Growing up alone, without a family, Todd had felt cheated by fate because it was something that was beyond his control. But now things were different. While he knew that nothing would ever come close to replacing the loss of his parents, he knew that he now had it in him to create a family his family; a family to love and cherish and spend the holidays with.

It didn't matter that she was an heiress to a multi-million dollar empire and he was lawyer striving to make partner. It wasn't something he even considered. She was so removed from the social circle she belonged to, it was so easy to ignore the difference. As far as he was concerned, Katherine was his family and that was it. His arms tightened around her and he let his mind and his body relax.

"I love coming out here," Katherine said softly after a while breaking the silence. A soft smile played on Katherine's lips as she recalled the summers she and her family had spent Hamptons. "It's beautiful, isn't it?" She pulled away slightly to glance at him when he didn't answer. His head had fallen back and he was fast asleep.

"Todd, Todd," she shook him gently.

He opened his eyes confused. "Did i...?"

She nodded. Todd groaned.

"Get up," she said straightening and holding out a hand. Todd followed her through the house. "Where are we going?"He asked as she led him up the stairs. She just smiled as she led him to a bedroom down a wide hallway.

Todd's eyes widened as looked around the room noticing pictures of her and what appeared to be friends and family on the white chest of drawers. The walls were covered with soft lilac floral wall paper and there were pieces of antique looking accessories on the white dresser. The white wrought bed with the lavender bedding looked so comfortable. "This is your room." he said incredulously.

"Yes, but don't worry your virtue is safe. I won't get you drunk and have my way with you."

"Damn!" he said with exaggerated disappointment. Katherine laughed.

She opened a wardrobe and pulled out a hanger. "Jacket." he looked at her blankly. "Give me your jacket." He took off his jacket and handed it to her. She hung the jacket on the door knob. "Now take off your shoes."

"Oh, I love it when you talk dirty," Todd said with a grin as he sat on the edge of the bed and kicked off his shoes and peeled off his socks. Todd was curious, he wanted to see where she was going with this.

Katherine rolled her eyes when he wagged his eyebrows. She walked over to the bed and pulled back the covers. "Why don't you get some rest?"

"I have a meeting in the morning," he reminded her.

"That's why you're going to set your alarm so you can leave early."

The offer sounded so tempting. He was dead on his feet. It had been a long day. He had been hoping to leave the office earlier, but he had gotten an urgent fax from a client which he simply couldn't ignore. He had ended up staying at the office two more hours. He wanted to spend as much time with Katherine as possible before driving back to the city, but his eyes seemed to be getting heavier by the minute. Maybe it would be a good idea to rest for a couple of hours.

"I guess I could take a load off for a couple of hours. But you have to stay and keep me company."

"I'll be back promise."

By the time Katherine returned with her mobile phone, Todd had begun to nod off. "Hey, come here," he said his voice groggy and his eyes heavy with sleep. Katherine switched off the lights before kicking off her shoes and joined him on the bed.

"So much for my grand romantic gesture," he mumbled his breath warm on her neck.

"Was that what that was?" she asked letting herself relax against his chest, feeling more peaceful than she had in a long time.

"Yeah, I was planning on driving down here and sweeping you off your feet."

"You *did* sweep me off my feet," she said her eyelids beginning to droop. She hadn't realized how tired she was. "Before you fell asleep and started snoring."

"Liar," he said giving her a playful nudge.

She laughed. "I'm glad you came," she said.

"Me too," he said with a sigh as they both drifted off to sleep.

Todd would have loved nothing more than to sleep in, but when he glanced at the bed side clock early the next morning he knew he had to go. He needed to rush back to town, take a shower and head for his meeting. He pulled away from Katherine reluctantly, hating to wake her but he couldn't bear to leave without saying good-bye. He watched her sleep as he shrugged into his clothes. She was breathtaking, with her hair splayed out on the pillow and her lips slightly parted.

"Katherine?" he whispered, leaning over to brush a soft kiss on the corner of her mouth. "I have to go." Her eyes went flying open as she went from deep slumber to full wakefulness in an instant. She stared at the ceiling, blinking several times as if to clear her head. Finally, she turned her head to look at him.

"Todd?"

"Expecting somebody else?" he asked with a laugh.

"What are you doing? Come back to bed," she said patting the mattress.

"I wish I could," he said sitting on the edge of the bed and leaning over to kiss her on the lips. "I have a meeting with the partners in a couple of hours." He said pulling away while he still could.

"You have to leave now?"

"Afraid so," he replied his heart warming at the forlorn look on her face.

"But it's so early."

"I know."

Katherine pulled the covers over her head and stamped her feet in frustration. "Ugh!" she exclaimed as she threw back the covers and got up heading to the bathroom. Todd couldn't believe it. Did the unflappable Katherine just throw a mini tantrum?

Todd chuckled. She sure wasn't kidding when she said she wasn't a morning person.

She emerged after a few minutes in a dark blue tank and matching drawstrings shorts. Her hair was pulled back in a ponytail and her face had been scrubbed of its make up. She looked so sweet and innocent. He could tell that she was embarrassed by her earlier outburst from the way she avoided his eyes. He reached for her and Katherine felt her embarrassment melt the moment their lips met.

"Oh no, you don't," she said pushing him away when he tried to deepen the kiss. "Not with that morning breath."

"Oh, you wound me," Todd said clutching his heart in mockery.

She laughed and darted back in the bathroom. "Here, this might help," she said handing him a new toothbrush. "I'll be in the kitchen when you're done."

57

"Can I get my morning kiss now?" Todd said when he finally found his way to the kitchen.

"Sit," she ordered.

"Did anyone ever tell you that you're bossy?" he asked in an amused voice as he settled at the kitchen table.

"Did anyone ever tell you that you had lousy timing?" she shot back as she cracked two eggs. As glad as she was that he had showed up, Katherine was still upset that he had to leave so soon.

He laughed as watched her add spices to the eggs and begin whisking them furiously. "You really aren't a morning person," he muttered under his breath.

Before long Katherine laid down his breakfast. His mouth watered as looked at the meal before him-cheese omelet, bacon, toasted bagels, a bowl of fruits and a steaming cup of coffee. She sat down next to him nursing a glass of orange juice while he wolfed down his breakfast. It felt so natural sitting at the breakfast table together chatting easily. It was as if they did that everyday.

"That was perfect," he said as he drained that last of his coffee.

"Well, I *am* a bit of a mind reader," she said with a mischievous glint in her eye she reached for his hand. She began to trace the lines of his palm, "I can see that you like your coffee with lots of cream."

"You're making fun of me," he said remembering his cheesy line from the park.

She laughed dropping his hand. "Katherine you and I can be good together. I feel it I know you feel it too," said in a poor imitation of his voice. "You have to admit that was kind of cheesy." she said with a giggle.

He looked at her thoughtfully before clasping both her hands in his. She tried not to wince at the pressure his hands were exerting on hers. Her laughter died at her lips and she wondered at his sudden change of mood. She found herself blushing at the intensity of his gaze but she couldn't to seem to pull away.

"It's true, you know. You and I *are* good together." He paused to gauge her reaction, but her face gave away nothing. His chest expanded with the deep breath he took. He looked at her hands in his, so small and fragile in comparison to his yet he knew that it in that that he would draw his strength, the strength to be a better man.

Todd knew that he was taking a risk baring himself to her like that, it was a risk he was willing to take. He was not about to play games with who could potentially be the most important person in his life. His eyes rose to meet hers. "Katherine, I love you." He said the words that had been burning at the back of his throat since he woke up that morning. He heard her inhale audibly. "You don't have to say anything. I just wanted you to know."

Katherine followed him to him quietly, her heart singing. He loved her! It hadn't all been in her head. He really did love her!

58

When they got to his car, Todd drew her close holding her to him like he would never let go. "I meant what I said back there. I love you," he said.

Katherine pulled away looking deep into his eyes. "I love you too," she whispered.

He smiled then and Katherine thought that not one had ever looked at her with such tenderness.

Chapter Seven

Seven Years Later...

An agitated Katherine looked across the table at her husband. It had been six years since they'd gotten married, bought a house and moved to the suburbs, keeping an apartment in New York.

The house had been a dream come true for Katherine. The large five bedroom duplex sat on a quiet street lined with sprawling lawns, immaculately kept gardens and big oak trees. Being the last house on the street, their home enjoyed more privacy, and had the biggest garden and a large shed, which they converted into an apartment for the live-nanny.

Like most of the houses in the area, theirs too had a wide front and back porch, a huge kitchen and living area. Katherine had fallen in love with the house the minute she'd laid eyes on it. She loved the white picket fence, the trees dotting the property and the impressive fire places the house boasted of.

She had envisioned their children running around freely, climbing trees and playing catch in the backyard. The artist in her had welcomed the challenge of turning the run down house into the cozy home she'd always wanted. It had taken her almost two years to complete the house to her satisfaction and when she was through, the result was breath taking.

The backyard was decorated in Japanese style, complete with a gazebo, a small koi pond and a little bridge. She had beautiful flowers everywhere. The front yard had a winding cobbled path leading from the picket fence to the front door. There was an arbor, a trellis and garden benches in the midst of a luscious garden. The house's décor combined French renaissance with a homey-country feel to it.

She loved her massive kitchen with its large French windows, the pots hanging over the island and the breakfast table big enough to sit six people comfortably. It was the heart of the house. Her second favorite room in the house was her closet. Knocking down the walls of the smaller bedroom next the master bedroom, turning the five bedroom house into a four bedroom, she transformed it into an exact replica of her closet in her New York apartment. Todd had been more than happy to take the smaller walk-in closet that came with the house.

Katherine had been so proud of her work, she would find herself beaming as she walked through the house. Now she was just bored. She longed for the days when she had barely enough time to think-poring over drawing and new ideas and taking care of twins.

Now that the house was done, the twins had started school and she had gotten a live-in maid, there simply nothing to do. Katherine knew that she should be happy. She was married to a handsome and successful lawyer, had two beautiful daughters and was living in her dream home. But she wasn't.

She felt as though the excitement and the life had been drained out of her, especially now that Todd seemed to be spending more time in the city. She sighed as the shrill sound of his phone ringing filled the room. This was supposed to be their weekend together. She hoped that he was not going to answer his phone, but she knew that that was too much to ask for.

With Todd, work always came first. The drive and passion she used to admire now irritated her. He promised her that he would slow down, maybe even take some time off so they can finally go on that family holiday. He'd take the kids to Disney world and then afterwards he and Katherine would go relax in the south of France.

So far, that that was all they had been. Promises. Katherine had gotten tired to listening to his empty promises. She had gotten tired staying up late waiting for him to come home from the city. Even the twins given up on him-they no longer expected him to be there to tuck them in at night or to take them to the park as he used to. Not wanting to be the nagging wife, she kept silent.

"Sorry hon, I gotta take this." He said with an apologetic look after glancing at his phone.

"Of course you do," she said. She watched him calmly as he rose from the table and walked to the adjoining living room talking in hushed tone.

"I'm really sorry Katherine, "he said when he hung up. "I have to go back to the Chicago tomorrow morning."

"I thought you said, you'd taken the week off."

"I have, but something came up in the office and..." his voice trailed off at the crestfallen look on her face. "I'll be back as soon as I can," he assured her. He hadn't taken time off work in a long time and he knew that Katherine had been looking forward to having him home for a change, not just her sake but their children's.

"The twin's recital is on Friday," she said in a pleading voice.

"I know."

"You can't miss it. You've missed so much already."

"Look, I said I'll be there, alright!" he snapped. Todd felt bad for snapping at his wife. He had a lot on his mind. And having Katherine sitting there judging him was not helping matters. "Katherine, I ..."

"I'd better go check on the girls," Katherine interrupted rising from the table and brushing past him. She should be angry but wasn't. She wasn't even disappointed. She was used to the disappointments, she almost expected it. The last couple of years had been full of them.

She wondered at how much he had changed. How much they had both changed. She remembered how they used to laugh and joke around and gaze at each other with love in their eyes. They had fallen in love so quickly and had not wasted time any time in getting married and starting a family.

They moved in together a year after they met. Less than a year later, Todd made partner and they were married. Life had seemed like a fairy tale. Katherine had gotten pregnant almost immediately. They bought a house in the suburbs and Todd convinced Katherine to close her business.

Katherine had not minded at the time, she wanted to be there for her kids the way her mother was when they were kids. She didn't want to miss a minute of watching them grow up. She wanted to take them to school, attend every recital and be an active member of the PTA and she knew that that would not be possible with the kind of business she ran.

Despite her family and friends' objections, Katherine sold part of her business to her former assistant, staying on as silent partner. She moved to the suburbs and proceeded to make a life for her budding family.

For the first three years, life was good. Todd was every bit the doting father and husband he'd promised Katherine he would be and Katherine tried to squash the feelings of regret she felt for having decided to be a stay-at–home mom. Over time however, resentment started to build up as Todd began to work longer hours and the novelty of being a stay-at-home mom wore off. Todd began to stay in their city apartment coming home only for the weekends, or sometimes not coming at all.

In an effort to keep them from drifting apart, Katherine would make plan to spend quality time together-plans Todd always seemed to break. She made her way slowly to the children's room where she settled into rocking chair. It is time I took control of my life, Katherine decided as she watched her daughters sleep.

As much as Todd was looking forward to spending his much needed vacation with his family, he had to go back to Chicago. He needn't bother explaining the situation to Katherine, because he knew that she wouldn't be interested. He told himself that the real reason why he didn't go after her was because she was clearly upset and he wanted to give her time to cool off.

The truth was, he was sick and tired of apologizing and even more so of the look in her eyes whenever he did; Katherine had lost faith in him and that hurt like hell.

Although she did not stir when he came in the bedroom they shared, Todd knew that she was wide awake. He already knew the drill. Katherine lying on the far side of the bed with her back turned to him meant one thing and one thing only. She was not interested in anything he had to say and he could forget about getting lucky tonight.

Great! *She nags about spending quality time together, but when I am home, all I get is the cold shoulder,* Todd thought as he got ready for bed.

She seemed indifferent to his presence, something that irritated Todd to no end. She didn't respond to him the way used. Her apathy led him to wonder-not for the first time-if she had met someone new. But he knew that that was very unlikely. Katherine was every bit as desirable as she had been when he met her and turned heads wherever she went, but she was also a principled person. He held on to the hope that she would never compromise herself by having an affair. There were the girls to consider. He hated to disappoint them.

TODD WAS NOT LOOKING forward to seeing his biggest client, Benjamin Goodman. The man had taken a special liking to Todd, something that paved the way towards helping Todd become a partner at the prestigious law firm. Goodman insisted on dealing only with Todd and had even made him several offers to come and work as his private council.

Although the offer had been very tempting, Todd had declined. He valued his freedom too much. Goodman was very demanding client. He was constantly looking for loopholes in the system. He thought he could bend the law at will and get away with it-and thanks to Todd, he always did.

Of late, Todd was getting tired of cleaning up after Goodman. He was beginning to feel less and less like a corporate lawyer. His conscience was beginning to catch up to him. Todd had always prided himself at being a principled man, but he could see the shreds of those principles flying out the window-he had become what he hated the most. He had become a suit.

I can't go on working for Goodman, he thought as he made his way through the airport departure lounge. *The man is a cess pool.*

The last case he handled for Goodman had been a very personal and delicate one. Todd had gotten a call from Dwight, his source at the Chicago Police Department, informing him that his client was yet in another scrape. The policeman had recognized Goodman's maid the minute she walked into the station.

Dwight had seen her a few times at Goodman's house. Maria was a very attractive woman in her late thirties. She had arrived with her teary-eyed 13 year old daughter. She claimed that Goodman had sexually abused her daughter and that she wanted to press charges.

Dwight had listened sympathetically, taking notes. He took her phone number and told her to go home and not worry. He would make preliminary investigations and get back to her. He had called Todd immediately. Todd's first reaction had been to hang up on Dwight and call Goodman and tell him he cannot represent him anymore. He fumed as he listened to Dwight recount what had happened, but the lawyer in him asked the appropriate questions. Apparently the girl had gone to the Goodman's after dance class to see her mother when he Goodman had groped her inappropriately.

"So she gave a statement?" Todd asked, the lawyer in him taking over.

"No, she thought she did. The station was pretty crowded so no one noticed."

"Thanks for the heads up, Dwight." Todd hung up feeling a little shaken. A 13 year old! He knew that Goodman was sleazy, but ....

When he confronted Goodman, Goodman was both surprised and outraged. "A 13 year old, for God's sake! Todd, you know better than to believe that story." He went on to tell Todd that Maria had stolen his wife's jewelry and they were contemplating whether or not to fire her. His wife, Nancy a sweet lady that Todd always liked confirmed the story.

Despite the warning bells that went off in his head, Todd believed him. He had done what he had to do to protect his client, vowing that it was the last time he saved Goodman from himself. And now here he was on his way to yet another rescue.

As he slid into the back seat of the limo Goodman had sent to pick him up at the airport. "Where's Raoul?" he asked referring to the driver Goodman usually sent. Todd liked Raoul. Raoul had a great sense of humor and always seemed to lighten up his mood.

"Raoul's at the funeral, sir," the chauffeur answered glancing at the side mirror as he pulled out.

"Funeral?" Todd hoped that it wasn't his mother. He knew how close the old man was to his ailing mother.

"Yes, sir. His cousin Maria lost her daughter last week."

Not one for idle chit chat, especially with one of his client's employees Todd mumbled his regrets and went back to the magazine he'd been reading on the plane. He'd barely gotten through the first paragraph when the chauffeur's words sung in. Fear gripped Todd.

No, it couldn't be. It had to be one a coincidence except, Todd didn't believe in coincidences. Over ten years of being a lawyer rid him of that and made him wary, very wary. His mind reeled at all the possibilities. Could Goodman have had anything to do with it?

The man was hardly a saint and seemed desperate to keep the story away from the media. Could he have been desperate enough to have taken drastic measures? If there was anything Todd had learned as an intern in the state prosecutor's office, it was that when it came to secrets, people where often desperate enough to do anything.

Katherine had always said that he would woe the day that Goodman that he agreed to represent Goodman. Even then, a part of Todd had known that she was right. This is probably the day, he thought, pinching the bridge of his nose. "Maria?" his voice came out harshly.

"Yes, she used to work at the mansion, sir,"the young driver glanced at Todd's reflection in the rear view mirror, puzzled at his sudden interest.

"How did she die?"

"Sir?"

"The kid, how did she die?" Todd grounded out.

"I'm not really sure, sir."

Todd raked his hands through his hair. His head felt like it was about to explode. "Do you where the funeral is?" he leaned over and asked.

"Yeah. It's at..."

"Take me there."

"But sir," the driver began alarmed at Todd's outburst.

"I said take me there," Todd yelled.

Todd's heart sank as he stood several feet away and watched the small coffin being lowered into the ground. He noticed Maria as she stood over her daughter's grave, looking broken. It looked like she was about to hurl herself onto the descending coffin. Todd felt like doing the same thing. He stood there frozen till the crowd started to disperse. His feet seemed to move of their own free will taking him closer to the grave.

He had to see for himself, he had to make sure that he wasn't dreaming. The poor kid had probably been molested by Goodman. He had known Goodman for long enough to know that his taste ran towards the young and the exotic looking. Deep down inside he had known that the girl was telling the truth and he had done nothing to help.

Instead, he threatened her mother and made her out to be a liar. And now she was dead. There was nothing he could do to change that. Maria paled visibly when she glanced back at the grave and spotted Todd.

"How dare you come here?" she shrieked in her heavily accented English approaching him. She lunged at Todd grabbing the collar of jacket, screaming in Spanish. "Haven't you animals done enough?!" She pounded his chest clawing at him until she was finally pulled away by Rauol. "She was just a child," she sobbed shaking uncontrollably.

He could still remember the little's girls brown eyes as she tripped over her words recounting what had happened. He remembered how brutal he had been. Badgering her with question after question till he finally confused her.

"Ms.lopez, I'm a lawyer. I'm only asking her questions she'll be asked in court. There are inconsistencies in her story, there's no evidence, no witnesses... I'm sorry. You don't have a case," Todd had explained carefully.

"But he has to pay for what he had done," Maria had sputtered desperately.

"Maria, you admitted to stealing Mrs. Goodman's bracelet. She could still press charges."

"But..."

"Mrs Lopez, with no concrete evidence or witnesses, it will your word against his. All the jury will see is a spiteful woman trying to even with her employee for getting fired," he interrupted gently.

"But that is not true!" Mrs. Lopez wailed. She looked at Todd wide-eyed and then at Dwight, and back to Todd. "I thought you were going to help us," she said, sounding both hurt and bewildered.

"I am here to help you," Todd had assured her gravely. "I am here to save you from making a big mistake. Now, you can take this retirement bonus and forget this whole thing ever happened or you can spend your entire savings on a case, I guarantee you, you will lose."

Maria Lopez started to get up.

"Mrs. Lopez, please," he said handing her a check. She glanced at the check and looked up at Todd, shocked, hesitated for a moment and started heading for the door.

"Mrs. Lopez, who would take the word of a child over that of an upstanding member of the community?"

"I believe my daughter," Maria spat out.

"I know you do, but like I said there's no evidence, no witnesses. It'll be her words against his. This will never make it to court, and even if it did. It could drag on for years. You'd end up spending everything you have on lawyers."

Maria paused at the door and she turned around to face him. "We both know how much you need the money. Think about the kind of life you could give Selena with this money," Todd rose from his seat and came to stand before her. Maria Lopez looked at him uncertainly. "You can put this behind you. It'll be as if it never happened," Todd added knowing that his work was done and that Maria Lopez would take the money. He was right.

Todd trudged back to the limo feeling completely numb. In his heart of hearts, he had known that Goodman was guilty and that Mrs. Goodman's willingness to fork out $20,000 wasn't entirely out of charity; it mostly had to do with keeping their names out of the papers. He should not have let her talked him into going to Maria and buying her silence. Todd felt manipulated and ... used. Goodman knew that Todd had a soft spot for his wife and admired her for charity works. He had probably put her up to it.

"I just wish I hadn't told John about the bracelet. You know how upset he gets about this sort of thing," she had told him in hush tones. "He would never let me keep her on. Poor Maria. And those girls. How will she survive with no job?! Todd you must help me make this right!" she had pleaded. Todd had bought the whole act. He fell for it hook, line and sinker. Now Selena was dead and her story would never be heard.

"Take me to the hotel," he said the chauffeur in a resigned voice.

"Sir?" the chauffeur looked confused. He was supposed to take him to the mansion.

"Take me to the closest hotel," Todd said through clenched teeth.

Chapter Eight

Todd dragged himself into the suite and threw himself on the bed, staring at the ceiling. He reached his coat pocket, pulled out his phone and switched it off. He needed to be alone. Todd squeezed his eyes shut trying to do away with the image of Selena's coffin being lowered to the ground. He eventually fell asleep. The persistent knocking on his door woke him up. Groaning, he got up and went to open the door. Goodman must have sent his watch dog get me, Todd thought bitterly.

He wasn't surprised when he swung the door and found Susan Whitman, Goodman's personal assistant standing there. She wore a tight black cashmere turtle neck sweater with a gray pencil skirts that stopped above the knee with black high heel pumps. Her wheat blond hair was pulled back in tight bun. She carried a large tote which he was sure held papers Goodman wanted him to take a look at. She walked past him into the suite without a word.

"Here," she said extending a thick file towards him. "Mr.Goodman wants you to take a look at these."

"You can leave them on the table."

She glared at him but dropped it at the table and sat down in a chair crossing her legs. "And you can fix me a drink and tell me what the hell is going on with you?"

"Susan, I'm not in the mood. Please leave," Todd said in a deadly voice still holding the door open and giving her a pointed look.

"Not until I get my drink," she said.

Todd slammed the door shut went to the mini bar, grabbed a bottle of water and tossed it at her. "Now get out."

She laughed unscrewing the cap slowly and taking a swig. She was aware that Todd hated her overt attempts to flirt with him and treated her with the same indifference rich people treated their butlers, something that annoyed her to no end. Today he was angry, anger she could deal with. She unwound her long legs and crossed the room to stand before him. One minute Todd was trying to shove Susan out the door, the next they were all over each other ... kissing.

It took the shrill sound of Susan's mobile phone to jolt Todd back to his senses. He managed to unclasp her her hands around his neck pushed her away from him. "I'm sorry. I cant do this," he said running his hands through his hair.

Susan laughed triumphantly. "Of course you can," she said approaching him.

"Susan, please leave," he said quietly.

"I don't think so," she purred.

"Fine, stay. I'll leave. Good bye, Susan." He walked out without looking back. He couldn't get out of there fast enough. The guilt he felt the day before came crashing down on him, hitting him like a ton of bricks. As he walked to the elevator, he tried to push away the memories of the last few minutes. Despite the problems between them, Todd had never cheated on Katherine. He had held himself back, knowing that she would never forgive him if he did. *What have I become? Maria was right, I'm no better than Goodman or the rest of the scumbags I defend, I am an animal!*

"Hey, it's really great to see, ya," Josh repeated for the second time since he'd ambushed Todd in the lobby outside the elevator. It'd been almost two year since they'd seen each other. Josh had surprised everyone by falling in love with a plain looking dentist and moving to Chicago. They had all been sure that it was a phase but four years and two kids later, Josh and Stacey were still going strong. Todd noticed that Josh looked happy. Really happy.

"Good to see you too, man," Todd replied trying to muster more enthusiasm. The last t thing he needed was a reminder of the good old days and the person he used to be.

"What brings you to town? Let me guess, Goodman?"

"Yeah."

Just then the elevator opened and Susan stepped out. "There you are," she said. "Make sure you look over those papers, will you. I'll send the limo down at 9:00. She brushed past Todd winking at him.

Todd stiffened when Josh stared at him and then turned to stare at Susan's retreating figure. "My meeting's not for another thirty minutes. Come on, I'll buy you coffee," Josh offered. Todd nodded hoping that his friend was not about to ask him for all the gory details.

"What the hell are you doing, man?" Josh blurted after their drinks had arrived.

"Excuse me?" Todd almost choked on his capuccino.

"Come on, man. I'm not blind."

"It's not like that. She's my client's PA."

"Todd, don't bullshit a bull-shitter, man." Josh hesitated before continuing. "Katherine doesn't deserve this."

Todd couldn't believe that this was coming from Josh. Josh had never hidden his skepticism at the notion of remaining faithful in marriage.

71

Reading his thoughts josh leaned over saying, "I know that this is coming as a surprise hearing this from me. Stacey has changed me. I have never been happier. Besides, it's Katherine we're talking about here. Whatever it is you're doing, it's not worth it, trust me."

"I told you it's not like that." Todd felt like a heel for lying to his best friend. Lately the lying had become so easy, almost second nature.

Josh studied his friend for a moment. "How *are* things with you and Katherine?"

Todd sighed. "Things haven't been good for a while. It's not just her, it's work and ..." he ran his hands through his hair.

"You know that you'll never find anyone like her if you lose her don't you?"

He sighed again. "I know."

"Whatever the problem is, it's not going to fix itself. Go home, Todd." Josh rose dropped a few bills on the table. "Hey, it's been great seeing ya. Give me a call next time you're in town." Josh rushed off to his meeting leaving Todd with memories of a better time.

"You know, honey, things are going to be different for us from now on," Todd said excitedly. He'd just been made partner at the prestigious law firm he'd been working for the last five years.

"Things are fine right now," she said chuckling. Todd's enthusiasm was infectious.

"Well, things are going to be better than fine, they're going to be great." He pulled her in his arms spinning her across the living room. "I'm going to get you a big house with a huge bathroom and a great custom-made closet and designer dresses, lots of designer dresses and a maid. You can finally quit that job..."

"I love my job. And you know I don't need those things." And she didn't. Katherine had been surrounded by luxury all her life, waited on all her life, had the best of everything but she never come close to being as happy as she had been this past year. She hadn't minded leasing out her much larger apartment with the fantastic view and the great walk in closet to move in with Todd. She loved waking up next to Todd every morning. She loved her job and was looking forward to starting a family of her own.

"We can finally get that house in the suburbs and start a family."

Katherine smiled. "That's the best thing you've said all night."

He took both her hands in his looking into her eyes he said, "You, know, I couldn't have made it without you. I don't deserve you. I never did. But I will..."his voice broke "I will try to make myself worthy..."

Katherine put a finger over his lips. "Don't ever say that." She cradled his face in her hands. "I love you Todd

Jenkins. That's never going to change," she told him fiercely her eyes misting over.

"I love you too," said Todd solemnly. *Gently he pulled her hands from his cheeks and kissed them. "That will never change, he vowed, "we will never change."*

They had changed though. Todd had let wealth and power get to his head. He had become so absorbed in his work and keeping up with the Jones's that he lost touch with who he was. He took on clients against his better judgment. As the size of his retainer grew, his conscious and sense of principles diminished. He started spending more time in his apartment in the city going to the suburbs to visit with Katherine only on weekends. Katherine lost faith in him and withdrew inward till he couldn't reach her anymore. The laughter went out of their marriage and eventually so did the sex.

Now it seemed as though his world was crashing down on him. He knew that he had no one to blame but himself didn't make him feel any better. Draining his cup, Todd got up. It's time to go home he told himself.

Chapter Nine

Todd leaned against his desk at the study, looking out the window watching his wife play with their twin daughters. With their rosy cheeks, blond hair and toothy grin they looked more and more like their mother everyday even though they had his piercing blue eyes.

Kyla, five minutes older than Debbie, had her mother's quiet strength and determination. Debbie copied everything her older sister did with a mischievous gleam in her eyes. She was the more adventurous of the two girls. Todd longed to join them, to lift his girls up in the air and tickle them as his wife looked on. But he couldn't.

His relationship with Katherine had become strained at best. She still made his favorite meals, travel arrangements, entertained his guests and remembered his birthday. She was still as devoted a wife as she had been from the moment they'd taken their vows except she never looked at him the way she used. He couldn't blame her though. He'd changed so much, he was not who he used to be. He'd become someone he barely recognized.

Katherine glanced up and saw but she didn't return his wave instead she bent down and whispered something to the kids. The girls squealed in delight. Even though he could not hear them, he knew what they were chanting, as they ran to keep with their mother as she headed back into the house. "Daddy, Daddy!"

Todd moved away from the window and made his way to the huge living room with French doors that opened up to the garden.

"Daddy!" they squealed in delight running to hug him around the legs.

He reached down and lifted them up to his chest, one on each arm. They both wrapped their little arms around his neck burying their faces in the crook of his neck. Todd's heart felt like it would burst from the love he felt for his daughters.

He set the girls down carefully and leaned over to give his wife a kiss. Katherine twisted face quickly and the kiss landed on her cheek. The look she gave Todd a look that surprised him. He hadn't seen her express anger or any emotion whatsoever in a every long time. Now that she has, he didn't know what to make of it.

"I'd better to see about dinner." Katherine swiftly made her way into the house and headed to the bathroom. Watching Todd with the girls almost undid her. She didn't know whether she had the strength to go through with her decision. She was at the end of her tether.

She didn't know how long she could go on living a lie and pretending that she and Todd were the happy couple. She didn't know how long she could go on telling herself that Todd business trips were just that, business trips nothing else.

The cracks were beginning to show. Just the other day Kyla had asked said to her, "Why are you so sad mommy?" When Katherine told her that she wasn't sad, Kyla looked hurt and replied in a solemn voice, "You look just like Debbie looked like when Pokey went to heaven." Pokey, the family cat, was run over by teenager earlier that year. Debbie who had a fondness for animals had taken it quite hard.

Katherine wasn't surprised by the comparison. Kyla had always been very perceptive seeming wiser than her age, but the thought that her five year old daughter could see her mother's pain broke her heart. I have to do it, she told herself looking at the mirror. I have to do it for the girls.

She wasn't about to let her daughters grow up being victims of a bad marriage. She would move back to Connecticut to be closer to her parents. She would go back to work. It always did make her happy. But would that make her daughters happy? Seeing their parents divorced?

A part of her was still hopeful that Todd would change, that he would stop the cheating, spend more time with the girls and look her the way he used, with love instead of guilt. It's stupid to hope that things would get better, Katherine thought bitterly. When would enough be enough? Coming home early from his "business" meeting for his daughters recital was not a sure sign that he was going to change.

How many times had he started to change only to disappoint her again? Hot tears of humiliation started to well up in her eyes. I will not cry, she willed herself. I will not waste any tears on him. She blinked back the tears, straightened her shoulders and looked in the mirror. She looked like she always did. Poised, cool and confident. Hair parted at the side and pulled back in loose bun at the nape of her neck her white sun dress with the green bringing out her eyes.

No one would be able to tell that she was falling apart inside. No one but her daughter, that is. Taking a deep breath, Katherine went to the kitchen to tell the maid, Gladys, to make Todd's favorite for dinner. She did not feel like cooking tonight.

Todd couldn't forget the look Katherine had given him that afternoon. It took him apart to see her in pain. The last time he had seen that look was five years ago when her father told her that a tumor had been discovered in his brain and he would have to undergo surgery. Todd had never seen her in that much pain. She had leaned on Todd for support then, drowned her sorrows in his embrace. Now it broke his heart to see that he could be the source of such pain.

Later that night, Todd walked into the room slowly. He felt drained. He had buried his conscious long time, refusing to let himself feel guilty about anything. He could hear Katharine in the shower when he walked into the bedroom. He walked to the dresser picking up framed pictures of his daughters looking adorable in their princess Halloween costumes. He remembered that he had promised to take them trick-o-treating, but had gotten caught up in a meeting that by that he got home they were fast asleep.

As he put down the picture of the girls, it struck him that most of the pictures around the house were of

Katherine and the girls, only a few included him; another reminder of the fact that he was never there. He put down the picture angrily and picked up the one of him and Katherine.

They were much younger then. And happier. Katherine looked breath takingly beautiful in her mother's wedding gown as she smiled up at Todd who had a possessive arm around her. They had been so in love and were sure so sure that they would be together forever. He put it down and picked up another one. He was standing behind Katherine with his arms around her cradling her swollen belly. They both smiled into the camera.

"That's one of my favorites as well," Katherine's voice came behind him, startling him.

"Yeah," he answered without looking up. He couldn't bear to look at her and see that anguished look and know that he put it there. "We were so happy weren't we?"

Katherine sighed. "I know."

"What happened to us Katherine?" the question came out more like a plea.

Katherine sat on the bed leaning against the pillow, pulling her knees up. How many times had she asked herself the very same question? "Life happened, I guess. We grew apart, changed."

Todd didn't know how to respond to that. She was right. They had grown apart, they'd both changed. Katherine had lost that twinkle in her eye. She seemed almost reserved when she was with him. it was like there was a part of her that he simply could not reach. He remembered thinking that maybe she was in love with someone else, having an affair. But he had changed too. He had become cynical and pretentious. The very thing he hated the most.

"But we still love each other though?" he could her the desperation in his voice. He had to know whether Katherine still felt the same way about him as he did about her. What if she didn't love him anymore? What is she had fallen in love with someone else? He squashed the idea immediately. Katherine was too noble to ever cheat on anyone, even an undeserving bastard like him.

Todd knew Katherine well enough to know furrow of her brows that she had heard his silent question and was trying to decide whether or not to give him an honest answer. "Yes," she said quietly meeting his eyes for the first time. "I still love you."

Todd let out the breath he didn't know he'd been holding. "Katherine." Putting the frame down on the dresser with a clatter, he rushed to her side . He perched on the bed next to her reaching to take her hands in his and lifting them to his lips kissing them over and over again. She twisted tucking her knees under her. She inched closer to Todd and planted a kiss on his forehead.

Todd's heart melted and reached out to put his arms around her. He held onto her like a man drowning, burying his head in chest, he sobbed, "Oh Katherine,"he sobbed over and over again drenching her teddy with hot tears of humiliation. He thought about all the different ways he'd wronged her, hurt her and the twins. He thought about Selena, young Selena with her big brown eyes full of fear; he thought about how much he had wronged her. His shoulders shook uncontrollably, his breathing coming out a short gasps.

Katherine was shocked at Todd's outburst. She felt like her ribs would crack from the strength of his embrace. She put her arms around his neck and rested her cheek on his head as tears ran down her face wetting his dark locks. She wept for all they had and all they had lost. She wept for what she faced to lose if she were to place her trust in this man again. She wept for not having the strength to stop loving him. She wept for the fear of what tomorrow might bring-more disappointments.

They remained like that for a long time, locked in each other's embrace till both of them were all cried out.

"Sorry, you must be uncomfortable," Todd croaked pulling away from Katherine looking slightly embarrassed.

"It's okay."

Katherine felt completely drained. She knew that they had a lot talk about, but she certainly wasn't up to it that night and she had a feeling neither was Todd. She edged closer to the center of the bed laying her head on a pillow and stretching out. Todd laid down beside her not bothering to take of his shoes. He rested the weight of his body on one elbow and stroking her cheek with the thumb of his other hand.

They were both too exhausted to say anything. They simply stared into each other's eyes till Todd's arm began to go numb. Shifting his weight, he lay on his side winding one arm around Katherine's waist. Katherine closed her bloodshot eyes and turned on her side linking her fingers with his and nestling into his chest, she sighed and drifted to sleep.

Chapter Ten

Todd woke up feeling better than he had in a long time. He took a deep breath inhaling his wife's sweet scent. This is where I belong, he thought happily. When Katherine stirred in his arms and made a move to get up, Todd tightened his arms around her. They lay in silence till the girls stormed in a split second after knocking on door. Katherine sat up spreading out her arms to hug them. The girls jumped on the bed giggling and talking at the same time.

"Mommy, daddy fell asleep in his clothes and his shoes," Debbie said and her sister erupted into a fit of giggles.

"I know," Katherine said with a smile and scooted off the bed. "Who's up for mommy's special pancakes?"

"Me," the twins shrieked in unison.

Todd tickled the girls while Katherine disappeared into the bathroom. She emerged a long silk house coat with her hair loose about her shoulders. The girls immediately jumped up to follow her. "You coming?" she asked raising an eyebrow.

Todd nodded his heart racing. Maybe he and Katherine had a chance after all. "I'll meet you downstairs." Todd quickly brushed his teeth went to the kitchen to join his family.

He stood at the door watching his daughters chat happily as they ate their breakfast. Katherine sat at the kitchen table with them cradling a cup of green tea, looking pensive.

Although she was happy that Todd was home and for the first time in years they had actually connected, she couldn't help the feeling of apprehension that consumed her. What had brought this on? Was Todd in some sort of trouble or did he just have a sudden change of heart? She eyed him as he walked into the kitchen to fix himself a cup of coffee. They certainly had a lot of talking to do.

Later after they had both showered and Gladys had taken the kids to the neighbor's for their play date Katherine and Todd went into the living. Katherine sat down on the sofa, one arm resting on the arm the other holding a throw pillow to her chest. She crossed her legs, raised an elegant brow and said, "Well?"

Todd knew that that was his cue to start talking, to explain the craziness of the past couple of years. "I don't even know where to start." Todd was too wound up to sit down. He stood by the fireplace gazing at the pictures on the mantle piece.

"Why don't you start at the beginning?"

"I don't know what happened. One minute I was on top of the world, married to girl of my dreams, a partner at one of the country's best law firms, the next minute I'm lost." He paused and when Katherine made no move to respond he continued. "I lost my way somehow. I guess I got scared that I could lose everything so buried myself in my work. The funny thing is, I wound up losing everything anyway-you, watching the girls grow up,

78

myself!"

Todd ran his fingers through his hair in frustration. He came to sit down on the couch next to Katherine and proceeded to tell her everything-from the scumbags he defended, to the incident with Susan. He noticed Katherine's arm tighten around the pillow she held, her face hardening but once he had started talking he couldn't stop himself. He told her about Maria, how he'd convinced her to take the money and not press any charges.

"Todd, how could you? She was just a child. What if she had been one of our daughters? What if it had been Kyla or Debbie?"

"I know, I feel awful and I'm sorry... "

"I'm not the one you should be apologizing to." She walked to the door.

"Katherine...."

"I don't want hear it," she interrupted in a angry voice. "You go back to Chicago and you fix this, if you ever want to see me or the girls again."

Todd paled. She couldn't mean it. She's just angry.

"I mean it, Todd. You fix this or I'm done."

Todd swallowed as he looked out the window at the run down apartment building. "You sure you wanna get off here?"the cab driver asked waving a hand at the run-down building of the dangerous neighborhood.

"Yes, but wait for me." The cab driver gave Todd a long look then shrugged. The minute he stepped out the cab, Todd realized that he didn't actually have a plan. He had been so eager to make things right that he hadn't put much thought into what he was going to do once he reached Chicago. He had gotten Maria Lopez' address form Dwight, boarded the first flight he could get to Chicago and headed there.

Perhaps he might have been to hasty. Five menacing looking boys in their late teens sitting on the building's front steps eyed him, taking in his designer suit, expensive shoes, no doubt noticing the Rolex watch on his wrist. He walked around them slowly avoiding their eyes as he made his way up the stairs.

Once inside the building he took off his watch and shoved it in his pocket, he didn't need to call attention to himself. Todd stood in front of Maria's apartment sweating buckets. Maria answered the door after just one knock. As soon as she saw who it was she began to push the door shut.

"Mrs. Lopez please,"

"What do you want?"

"Can we talk? Please,"

"Why?"

"Listen, I'm really sorry about what happened. I just want to talk. Please."

"So what do you want?"she asked angrily cracking the door a little wider.

"I wanted to…" Todd's voice trailed off as he stared past her shoulders. It can't be. "Is that…?"

"You stay away from her," Maria warned and turned to yell at her daughter in Spanish. Todd stared at the girl as she disappeared into a bedroom. She started to close the door again.

Todd stuck his foot in the door to stop it from slamming shut. "I don't understand. I saw them bury her at the funeral. i…

Maria's hand went slack at the door and she sighed. "That was not her."

"I don't understand, "he repeated.

"It was her sister."

Todd was dumbfounded.

She sighed and opened the door wider to let him in the tiny apartment. He went in, glad to be out of the dark hallway.

"This is a very dangerous neighborhood, Mr. Jenkins," she said as she gestured to him to sit down.

"I know," he said.

"You shouldn't have come."

"I know."

She walked over to a table full of frames and picked up one of them. "This is Tanya; she was Selena's older sister."

"The coffin… Was she…?" he heart twisted as he looked at the picture of the frail young girl who looked so like her mother.

Maria nodded sitting down. "Tanya was very sick. She had cancer-leukemia- since she was six years old." She saw Todd glance back at the picture he was cradling. "She was small for her age. She was eight." Her eyes welled up with tears. "Mrs Goodman promised she would help me pay for her treatment," she told him her voice full of contempt. "But she lied. That was why I took the bracelet." She looked at him then. "I am not a criminal, Mr. Jenkins."

"I know."

"She was on the list to get bone marrow transplant. The doctor said it could have saved her. but there are so many people on the list and ... " her voice trailed off as tears streamed down her face.

"I'm so sorry," Todd said softly his heart going out to her.

Maria looked out the window struggling to compose herself. They sat in silence, the distant sound of siren and the sound of the clock ticking filled the apartment. She took a deep breath and turned to face him, her nostrils flaring out slightly in anger. "What is it that you want?"

"Mrs. Lopez, I am sorry for your loss. I am also sorry about what happened with Selena." He noticed her eyes narrow slightly in suspicion. "I should not have convinced you to take the money. It was unethical, not to mention unfair to you and Selena. I would understand if you still want to press charges."

She seemed to ponder what he said and then sighed. "That is okay. Perhaps you were right. It would be better if we just put this behind us and try to move on."

"Are you sure?"

"Yes," she said firmly. "It's okay. Actually, it's not okay, but at least now I have enough money to leave this god forsaken neighborhood and try and give my daughter a better life."

"You are a very strong woman, Mrs. Lopez." He said meaning it.

"And you are a brave man, for coming to this neighborhood dressed like that. I hope you did not come with your car."

"No, I did not."

"Good, because the rims, the stereo and the tires would've been gone by now." When she rose, he knew that his time was up. He got up and walked to the door.

"Maybe I better walk you down," she said.

He started to say it was not necessary then he remembered the young men sitting on the stairs, no doubt waiting to mug him and said, "I'd really appreciate that."

Todd slumped in the back seat of the cab not sure how he felt. He was sorry that Mrs. Lopez had lost her daughter. Another part of him felt glad that she had money to give her younger daughter a better future. He was ashamed at the guilt gnawing at him because he was relieved that she was not going to press charges. The last thing he needed was to get involved in anything that could get him disbarred. He pulled out his phone to call

81

Katherine to tell what had just happened, but he knew that she would not pick up his call. Not yet. He sent her a text message instead.

Chapter Eleven

Katherine was still angry when she woke up the next morning. She didn't even bother to read the note Todd had left her before he left. As she got ready for her morning run, she tried not think about how helpless the mother must have felt at not being able to do anything to defend her daughter or how betrayed her daughter must have felt at having her silence bought.

She couldn't believe that Todd was capable of such a thing. As much as she loved him, she just was not sure that she could live with him anymore. He used to be so honest so principled, she knew that he had changed a lot in the past five years, she just hadn't realized how much he had changed.

At least, he had come clean. That was something. She was surprised when he said he'd cheated on her for the first time. She knew that he wasn't lying about that. A part of her was relieved to find out that she had been wrong for the past three years, assuming that a woman, not his work, was the real reason he spent so much time in the city.

She had been so convinced that he was cheating on her that she froze him out. She couldn't bear to have him touch her especially since she was convinced that he had been with other women. She couldn't remember the last time they had had sex. But that did not give him the license to cheat on her.

Katherine spent a better part of the day fuming. His text message angered her even more when she finally got around to reading it. True, in an ironic twist of fate, Todd had actually helped Maria Lopez. But he still. What he did was wrong. He had not right to bully that woman into silence. He could have lost his license, something he'd worked so hard for. *If he thinks that apologizing to that woman makes everything okay, he's got another thing coming.*

Todd walked in the house carrying a bouquet of lilies and a basket. He felt silly holding the flowers since his house was already full of them. The basket held an assortment of cheeses, belgian chocolate and vintage wine, something he knew Katherine loved. He found her sitting in the gazebo sipping what he guessed must be green tea. He set the bouquet and the basket on the wicker table in front of her. She continued to stare ahead, ignoring him.

"I..uh.. brought you something," he said uncertainly breaking the silence.

"I can see that but as you can see, this house is full of flowers and I am trying to lose ten pounds. You would know that if you were around more often."

The few extra pounds that had remained after the twins only made her look more curvaceous and womanly. He loved that she filled out her jeans more. There was more to hold onto, as he like d to say. Todd opened his mouth to tell her that she looked great, but thought better of it. He waited for her to say something, but she continued to stare ahead, sipping her tea. "Katherine I am really sorry. I know I let you down."

"Yes you did."

"I have been under so much pressure. And I've been lonely..."

"You've been ...." Katherine paused and took a deep calming breath. Her face flushed in anger, Todd could see that she was struggling to control her temper. She glanced at the doorway and he knew that she was thinking of the girls. She didn't want them to hear them arguing. Lowering her voice she continued, "You've been lonely?! I'm the one who's stuck in the house all alone. And you're telling me that you've been lonely?"

"Katherine, I didn't mean...."

"I'm glad that you were able to straightened things out in Chicago," she interrupted. "Really, I am but I am not going to be a shoulder for you to cry on. I think I have been patient enough. You have to assume some sort of responsibility, here."

"Katherine if you would just listen..."

"No, you listen," she interrupted angrily sitting up and jabbing a finger in the air for emphasis. "*You* pushed me away, you had the affair, *you* chose to spend more time with your clients than your kids, *you* chose to represent Goodman even though you knew the kind of person he was. *You* pushed that lady into taking that check when you knew deep down that that little girl was telling the truth. *You* did. That was all you! So don't come in here expecting *me* to feel sorry for *you*."

"I know, believe me, I know. I just wish I could go back and do it all over again, but I can't. All I can do is try to make things right, with you, with the kids, with myself. I just need you to give me a chance. Let me make it up to you."

"Honestly Todd, I don't know if you can." Katherine set her mug down on the table with a clatter. "The twin's recital is in an hour, I need to get ready."

Katherine maintained a calm and friendly face throughout the ballet recital. He could tell from the clenched jaw and stiff back that he was no where near being off the hook. Despite the tension between them the evening went well. The girls were giddy with excitement that their dad was coming to the recital. Todd watched his daughters with pride wondering what had ever possessed him to choose work over spending time with them.

Todd paused at the door of his daughters' bedroom to switch of the light. He had just tucked them in, something he hadn't done in a long time.

"Thank you, daddy," Kyla's voice came through the partially dark room.

Surprised Todd asked, "what for?"

"For canceling your important business meeting and coming to our recital," said Kyla.

"Yeah and for tucking us in," Debbie chipped in

Since when did children have to thank their parents for being parents? He walked over to Kyla's bed and bent down to kiss her forehead. "You don't ever have to thank to thank me for being there. Ever."

"I'm happy you came," she said quietly.

"Me too."

"Me three," Debbie called out from her bed and after a moment's thought added, "And mommy too."

Todd was glad the room was dark and his daughter couldn't see the tears he could feel welling up in his eyes.

"I love you kiddo."

"I love you too, Daddy."

He walked over to Debbie's bed. "I love you Daddy," Debbie said exuberantly rising to press wet kisses all over her father's face. Todd tickled her and she fell back on her bed giggling.

"I love you too, princess."

"What are doing?" Katherine asked as Todd when he walked into their bedroom.

"I.."

"Did you think that I would let you waltz back in here just like that?"

"Well, I..uh... I thought... "

"Well, you thought wrong. You will stay in the guest bedroom till we sort things out," Katherine informed him in a tone that left no room for argument.

Red-faced, Todd quietly headed to the guest bedroom. He knew that he had not right to be angry, but he was. he was angry, hurt and humiliated. This was the first time Katherine had kicked him out of their bedroom. but then again, what did he expect. He had just let her in on how much of a scumbag he really was.

He should have seen it coming. Coming clean and going to Chicago to "fix"things with Maris wasn't going to score him any points. Of course she would kick out the bedroom, give him the silent testament all night and not bother replying his text messages. He was lucky she hadn't kicked him out the house!

Chapter Twelve

The next morning when Todd went to their bedroom to take fresh clean change of clothes before his morning shower, he noticed that a lot of his things were missing.

"What the…?"

"Morning," Katherine breezed as though nothing was out of the ordinary. "Oh, I moved some of your things to the other room. Thought it would be easier that way." She threw him a challenging look that let him know that if he wasn't happy with the current living arrangement, he could always leave.

Todd turned red with anger. "Fine," he said between gritted teeth. "Any other house rules I should be aware of?" he asked sarcastically.

"Yeah, take the garbage out."

"Doesn't Gladys always…?"

Katherine threw him another challenging look. They stared at each other angrily for a long time. He knew what she was trying to do. She wanted him to get angry and leave, but he was not about to do that.

"Garbage, got it. Anything else?" *You're not getting rid of me that easily.*

"No phones at the table or…"

"Don't worry about that," he said and walked to his side of the bed and pulled open the bedside drawer. Picking up his mobile phone and blackberry, both of which were switched off, he said, "See, mobile phone and blackberry on leave of absence." He dropped them back in the drawer and turned to look at her with a sardonic smile.

"Quit trying to be cute, Todd," she snapped. "It won't do you any good," she added and she stormed out the room.

Katherine ignored him for the rest of the day. She only spoke to him in front of the children. Even then, she didn't do it directly. She did it through the kids. The kids were so excited to have their father home, they did not notice that anything was amiss.

At least I'm sleeping in the guest bedroom and not a hotel, he thought. Todd spent the whole day thinking about how to resolve the situation. He knew better than to try and apologize. Buying presents would be futile. It would just irritate her the way his basket of goodies had the other day.

He knew that he had two things going for him. One: she still loved him and two: she was letting him stay in house. Katherine was very stubborn but he won her over before he believed he could do it again. The best course of action for him would be not to bring up any of the unpleasantness. He had a better chance charming her into forgiveness than he did groveling for it. Todd woke up the next morning with a clear since of purpose. Today is day 1 of Operation Charm Katherine. He jumped into his tracks and headed downstairs.

"What are you doing?" she demanded when he followed her out to the front porch.

"I am getting ready for a morning run. Same as you."

She glared at him. "What!! I'm not trying to be cute," he said holding up his hands.

"What are you trying to do then? Annoy the hell out of me?" Katherine was not a morning person and clearly today she had woken up on the wrong side of the bed.

"I just thought it would be nice if we did things together, you know try to reconnect."

She rolled her eyes, something she hadn't done in a long time. "You know what?" she sighed. "Just ... don't talk." She set off running.

Todd caught up with her. "Beautiful day isn't it?" he said. Katherine glared at him. "Right, right. No talking," he said.

She glared at him once more before increasing the volume on her i-pod.

Over the next 3 weeks Todd devoted his entire life to working on his marriage. He took much needed time off work. It had not been easy, but since he had pretty much worked for the past three years without taking a break, the other partners had to concede. He took his kids to summer day-camp, the park and went jogging with his wife.

Though Katherine had warmed up to him, she never let Todd near her again. I guess I'll be in here a while, he thought bitterly as he looked around his assigned room. Todd mauled over whether he should ask Katherine if he could move back to their bedroom, but decided against it. Things were going so well between them and Todd was not about to take any chances.

Katherine surprised him one morning during their morning run. She stopped half-way through the route they always took. He stopped concerned that maybe her leg was cramping. "Todd, what did you mean when you said that you were afraid to lose everything?"

"What?" he asked incredulously trying to catch his breath.

She leaned back on the bark of a tree, taking deep breaths. "The other night, you said that you were working so hard because you were afraid of losing everything. What did you mean by that?" she asked looking up at him.

Todd walked slowly to a nearby rock and sat on it. He looked at his hands for a long time. "Katherine, I'm not like you. I had to fight every step of the way for everything, knowing that if I allowed myself to slip even once, I could lose what I had.

"After my parents died and my aunt moved in to take care of me... I knew that I had to work hard. I had to work hard to stay in the high school I went to because I knew that aunt Celeste thought the school was too expensive and was looking for an excuse to send me to public school. I had to work hard to stay in college because I knew that she was looking forward to seeing me fail. I had to work hard to make good grades in law school so I could get a good job.

"And when I met you, I knew that I hard to work even harder." He looked up at her then. He could see the question in her eyes. "Katherine, I'm not blind. I know that I don't deserve you. The day you agreed to marry me was the happiest day of my life, but it was also the scariest. I was afraid every day that one day you would wake up and you would realize that maybe we rushed into things or that you made a mistake."

"How could you say that? You know how much I love you."

"I know, but I kept thinking, what if you begin to miss it. The life you had before. I know how much you love Europe and Aspen. I know how much you love vintage wine, and large closets and shopping for antique and attending auctions and ... all those things that have been a part your life. I knew that there was no way I could afford to give you those things without making partner and making sure that the business grew. I wanted to give you the same kind of life, someone like josh or Greg would have given you."

"But I didn't choose josh or Greg," she wailed. "I chose you."

"Exactly. You chose me." He took a breath. "if you had gone running to Josh or Greg all excited about a house that you just had to have, would either of them had said, 'gee hon, I'm sorry I can't afford it right now.'?"

Katherine blanched.

"Exactly."

"Honey, I had no idea..."

"Of course you had no idea. Money is not something you ever had to worry about."

Katherine could feel her face burning with shame. All those years and he never said anything. She remembered how excited she had been. She couldn't wait for him to come home. She had dashed to his office to meet him. "Oh honey, I just found us our dream home. It's absolutely beautiful. It's got a huge yard overlooking the lake, a huge porch and it's perfect. I just have to have it!" she had gushed. She hadn't even considered the cost.

"But why didn't you say anything?"

"Because I wanted to make you happy. I didn't want you to have any regrets. I wanted to give you everything you ever dreamed of. I wanted to give the house you wanted so you could decorate it the way you wanted. And it was worth it, for a while there you were happy... we both were. The girls came and it was great," he told her a sad smile playing on his lips.

"It was the happiest time of my life and I didn't want to miss a moment away from the kids or you... but there were bills to be paid." He sighed. "Having the babies, the house, the renovations... I had to work hard. I had to bring in more accounts. I had to stick with Goodman even though I couldn't stand the bastard. He was and still is one of our biggest accounts. I just had to. There was so much at stake. And I was afraid that I was losing you. The more scared I got the harder I worked. You just seemed to drift away and I could see the resentment and the regret in your eyes every time I looked at you. So I stayed away." He looked down at his hands again. He felt her hands on his shoulders and he looked up to her misty eyes.

"I did have regrets, Todd," she said softly. Todd felt as though his heart would rip into shreds. He nodded numbly. "None of them had to do with you. It's me. "

"It's okay, Katherine. You don't have to explain," he said rising and turning his back on her.

"No, I want to. I shouldn't have..."

"I don't understand, Katherine. Why were you so unhappy? You kept saying you had everything you ever wanted but you still seemed to ... withdrawn. I miss the old you. Your thirst for life, the way you used to laugh. You never laugh anymore." He looked at her puzzled, his eyes searching for answers in hers. "What happened?"

Katherine hesitated. "Loneliness, I guess. I have to admit, a part of me does miss my old life."

Todd nodded slowly.

"Not in the way you think though," she rushed on. "I miss waking up with a list of things to do, I miss not knowing how the day is going to end, I miss the challenges, the thrill, the... I miss working."

Todd's head snapped up. This was the last thing he expected to hear.

"Don't get me wrong, the first couple of years with you were great-the happiest in my life. I had the girls and I was working on the house and you were there. You always came home, no matter how busy your day was, you came home. But after a while you just stopped. The girls started school and were gone most of the day and the house was done and then you stopped coming home. I am always all alone in this big house."

"But I thought you wanted to be a stay-at-home mom. You said it was rewarding." Todd was shocked.

"I did, and it *is* rewarding, but I think... I need more."

"Why didn't you say anything?"

"I felt guilty and a little ashamed, I suppose. I knew that I should be happy. I mean, I had everything I ever wanted... but something felt missing. I thought that I could shake it off. But I can't. Besides, you were never home."

"I was never home because you didn't want me around."

"Of course I wanted you around," she wailed. She bit her bottom lip. "What was I supposed to do? All of a sudden you just stopped coming home and you had all these meetings and...."

"Whoa, wait a minute," he said interrupted and bolted to his feet. "You thought I was having an affair?!"

Katherine folded her arms across her chest and looked at Todd angrily. "Well, I wasn't wrong now, was I?"

"I can't believe this!" he paced angrily. "I kissed one woman, once! In seven years! Once!"

"I suppose you think you deserve some sort of medal!" she spat back angrily.

"You didn't exactly give me a reason not to!" he retorted.

"What's that supposed to mean?"

"You know exactly what I mean!" he snapped back glaring at her. "You've become this cold, unresponsive person I don't even recognize anymore." Katherine flinched at his choice of words but he was to far gone to notice. "When was the last time we actually made love?"

Katherine looked away from him.

"Eight months, Katherine! You haven't let me near you in almost a year," he said raising his voice.

"That's not true."

"Yes, it is," he said quietly striving to keep his temper in check. He knew how quickly things could get ugly and the last thing he wanted was to fight. He grabbed her elbow to stop her as she started to walk away. "Katherine, I love you but you can't keep freezing me out."

Katherine looked up into her husband's anguished eyes.

He took another deep calming breath and placing his hands on her shoulders and turning her to face him. "I promise you, the only reason I stayed away was because I couldn't bear to look in your eyes and see that look that said you didn't want me anymore."

Slowly Todd came closer and wrapped his arms around her. She didn't respond at first, she merely stood still and let him hold her. Slowly, she snaked her hands around his neck and buried her face in his chest. "I love you,

Katherine. I love you so much." He pulled away, cupping her face in hands, his eyes boring into hers. "I need you to believe me. There has never been anyone else ... apart from Susan. You're the only one I want."

"I believe you, Todd, but it's not enough," she said a in a sad voice breaking away from his embrace.

They walked the rest of the way in silence both of them immersed in their own thoughts.

Chapter Thirteen

A dark cloud seemed to over them throughout the rest of the day. Katherine refused to believe that they might have rushed into marriage and starting a family as family and friends seemed to suggest. She had acknowledge, however, the fact that as much as they loved each other, they did not communicate. It had been like that since the very beginning.

They had talked about everything-work, their dreams, their families, life growing up-but they had never talked about money and they had never talked about relationship. They loved each other, they understood each other and believed in each other and thought that that was enough to weather any storm.

Katherine had always sensed that Todd did not want to be reminded of the fact that he and Katherine had come from different worlds. He ignored the fact that she was an heiress and she pretended that she wasn't. When he suggested that they move in together, Katherine had been ecstatic. She didn't want anything to spoil how great things were going so she refrained from pointing out that her apartment was actually bigger, in a better location and that she owned it so they wouldn't need to worry about rent. She had simply put some of things in storage, leased out the apartment and moved in with him.

She had signed the prenuptial agreement he insisted her lawyers draft without batting an eyelid. She let him pay for trips and all the household expenses because she knew that he felt that it was his role as a man to do so. She had not wanted to rock the boat. May be she should have. It might have saved them both a lot of heart ache.

When Todd had started spending more and more time in the office, Katherine had tried not to complain. She had not wanted to be the nagging wife. She had not wanted to complain that she was bored. So she played the role of dutiful wife and mother. She began to resent the time Todd spent in the city. She would get angry whenever he would come home late after the girls had already gone to bed. She got angry every time he wasn't there to eat the gourmet meal she had spent hours toiling over. She got angry every time he came home too tired to make love. And each time, Katherine held her tongue. She did not want to be the nagging wife. The angrier she got, the more distant she became. As painful as it was to admit it, there was no denying the fact that Todd had been right. She did freeze him out. She was angry that everything had to be on his time. They only went out when he wanted to or spent time together when he could or made love when he wasn't tired.

Katherine never thought of herself as selfish or self-centered. Apparently, she was wrong. It broke her heart to think about how much pain she had inflicted on him. All those years she had been angry, punishing him, punishing them both and all he had been trying to do was make her happy. Fear gripped her as she realized that Todd had quite a bit invested in the stock market. What if he had lost everything? What if he hadn't pulled out in time?

Katherine jumped off her bed and began to pace the room. A lot of people hadn't seen what had happened in Wall Street coming. The financial melt down had crippled so many people's businesses. Heeding the advice of a friend, her father had pulled out most of his major investments before d-day and advised Todd and Katherine to do the same.

Try as she might, she couldn't remember what Todd's response to that had been. Maybe that was what had brought on this outburst of emotion, Katherine thought thinking of the night he had wept in her arms. Whatever it is, she prayed silently, we'll find a way of working it out. We have to, we love each other. Knowing that she would be unable to go back to sleep, Katherine decided to go down to the kitchen and make herself a hot cup of cocoa. She was surprised when she saw Todd rummaging through the refrigerator.

"Hi."

He looked up in surprise. "Hi." He held up a tub of chocolate-chipped ice-cream.

"I shouldn't," she replied thinking of her diet.

"Come on, live a little." He opened a drawer and pulled out two spoons.

Katherine walked over and took the spoon. They settled on the kitchen stools eating the ice-cream straight out the tub.

"Good isn't it?"

"Mmmm ," Katherine said as dug out a spoonful. "There goes my diet, "she murmured.

"From where I'm standing, you look great."

"Humph." Even as she grunted, Katherine couldn't help the warm glow she felt at the complement. This was the second time he'd said that to her today. She remembered how he used to look at her in reverence-like she was the most beautiful thing he had ever come across.

When she was pregnant, he would lift whatever she was wearing and caress her swollen belly, showering kisses all over it and telling her that she was absolutely the most beautiful pregnant woman there has ever been. After she had given birth to the twins and she told him that she was thinking of getting laser treatment to get rid of the faint stretch marks on her stomach, he had been horrified.

"Why would you want to do a thing like that? You got them giving us the greatest gift ever. They're a part of who you are now, kinda like battle scars," he had said tracing the faint white lines on her lower abdomen with his fingertips. "They're beautiful. Unless, you're really bothered by them, please don't get them layered off." After that she never looked at her stretched marks the same way again. That was what Todd had been like in the past. He made her see things in a new a light. He made her see herself in a new light. But that was then.

95

They ate the ice-cream in silence for a few minutes.

"I'm sorry about earlier," Katherine said putting her spoon down.

"Me too."

"You were right. I did freeze you out. You were always gone and I was angry and hurt... I thought you were having an affair."

"But I... "

"I know."

"It was stupid and it didn't mean anything," he said reaching out for her hand. "You're the only one I want." He leaned his forehead against hers his eyes questioning, waiting.

Although Katherine had been so relieved that he wasn't having an affair, she still felt angry and betrayed over the kiss. The logical part of her brain told her that she should move past it, but she couldn't honestly tell him that she's forgive him. "I'm sorry I doubted you, but I think I need more time," she said softly.

She heard him draw in a shaky breath. "I understand."

"We still have a lot to work out," she said straightening.

"I know."

They ate the rest of their ice-cream in silence and went to bed without exchanging another word.

Todd went over the events of the day as he crawled into bed. He felt most of the anxiety of the week seeping away. As least they had opened dialogue. Katherine had been stoic for so long it was good to finally see her show emotion-even if that emotion is anger.

He had no idea Katherine missed working or that she thought that he had been an affair in the city. That explained her coldness towards him. What if josh had been right? What if he had rushed her into marrying him? He had been so afraid of losing her, he had plunged into the relationship head on, suggesting that the move in together and then proposing shortly afterwards.

Being with her had seemed too good to true that he couldn't wait for them to start a life together. Looking back, maybe they had rushed into things, but there was nothing he could do about that now. He would focus on the fact that by some miracle she still loved him and had no regrets about having married him.

Deep down inside, Todd knew that making sure that he could provide her with the life she was accustomed to was not the only reason he worked himself to the ground. He still felt like he had something to prove. He had spent the better part of his life in the shadows of the likes of Greg-rich, sophisticated trust fund babies.

In high school, he watched his peers get whatever they wanted-girls, booze, drugs ... you name it. While they were busy partying, getting in and out of trouble and enjoying their youth, Todd spent most of his time alone alternating between track, his part-time job and studying. His friends from grade school had quickly distanced themselves from him after it came evident that his economic conditions had changed. And Todd found himself walking the school hallways alone. It was almost as if he were invisible. He wasn't bullied like some of the less privileged kids but he wasn't invited to any parties either.

Sometimes he would notice girls watching him with interest, but he knew that they would consider going out with him as "slumming it" so he ignored them. Then he met josh at Yale and everything changed. Josh took him under his wing and Todd was no longer invisible. He quickly became part of the gang, was invited to all the parties and girls threw themselves at him. But he was always painfully aware of the difference between him and his friends.

Although their arrogance and complete lack of regard for rules irritated him for the most part, Todd couldn't help but envy them their freedom. He longed for the kind of freedom that came with money. Knowing that he could buy whatever he wanted and still be secure in the fact that there was more where that came from. In his effort to capture that freedom, however, he had ended up almost losing the most important thing in life: his family.

Todd couldn't help but feel smug after he and Katherine had gotten married. If those girls could see me now..., he had said to himself thinking of the rich girls in high school that had been ashamed to be seen with him. Not only was Katherine beautiful and smart and funny, she was also ten times richer and classier than any of them *and* she was head over heels in love with *him*. Todd knew how lucky he was to have found Katherine. She made him feel so secure and he found himself opening up to her in a way he had never opened up to anyone. She filled that void that had been there since his parents died. Todd could not afford to lose her; not now, not ever.

He knew that she was still sensitive about the whole Susan-issue and it would take her time to loosen up, but at least she believed that it was his first and only offence. That was a start. He felt hopeful as he drifted off to sleep.

Chapter Fourteen

Katherine knew that she couldn't put off talking to Todd about their financial situation any longer. She felt guilt eating was away at her. She had never given much thought to how much the house had cost or whether Todd could afford it at the time or not. In fact, she had never given much to money in her life. It had always been there.

When she started her business, she was more afraid of the prospect of failing than at that of losing her investment. She bit her lip when she thought about the money she had spent on fixing the garden, renovating the house and buying antiques pieces "she just couldn't live without". Todd insisted on paying for everything and he never batted an eye when he saw the bill. What if it had been too much?

It suddenly struck her that she did not know exactly how much Todd made a year. Sure, she had an idea, but she was not sure exactly. They never discussed money. She was ashamed to admit that she had no idea what his savings were like or if he even had any. She simply let him pay for everything because she knew that he wanted to.

Occasionally she would go shopping with Ashley or treat herself to a spa treatment. Katherine knew that she was not a reckless spender. Unlike most of her friends, she found shopping to be a chore and no longer felt the need to keep with every season's trends.

She liked going to the grocery store and doing the cooking herself. She loved getting down on her hands and knees and fixing the garden herself. She no longer had to be chauffeured around in a limo. She was middle class for the first time in her life and she reveled in it. How could Todd not see that? If she was unhappy, it was because she was bored and lonely and sure that he was affair an affair with someone in the city. It certainly wasn't because she missed her old glamorous life.

"I think we need to start being honest with one another," she blurted out as they sat in the gazebo watching their daughters play on the swings.

Todd turned to look at her, surprised. "Katherine, I have never lied to you."

"What I mean is, we need to start being more open with one another. We can't choose to not to talk about certain things." She saw him nod. "We need to talk about money," she added hesitantly. Money was a sensitive issue for Todd-always had been. And from the way he stiffened, she could tell that it still was.

"Our finances are intact. You don't have to worry about that," he said turning slightly red.

"That's the point, Todd," she said twisting in her seat to face him. "Don't you see? I do need to worry about that." He turned to face her, his expression wary. "You're right. You and I come from very different backgrounds. Money was something I never had to worry about. That was then."

"I told you…"

"Look, I need you to stop telling me what I can and cannot worry about. Now, we need to talk about our finances, because that is what it is…ours. I need to know exactly what our financial status is so I know my budget is. We can't let the same thing that happened with the house happen again, especially with the recession going on. I need to know whether I am overspending or not." He looked away slightly uncomfortable.

"Todd, when we got married, you insisted that I sign a prenup. You made me promise me to always come to you if I wanted anything. And I did because I trusted you. Now you have to trust me. This is the only way this is going to work."

"Fine, but just so you know, our finances are doing great," he assured her drily.

"Good. But I still need to be in the know."

Todd sighed. "I guess that sounds reasonable."

"And um… also… Honey, I was wondering… I mean the stock market…"

Todd smiled as Katherine fumbled knowing what she was trying to ask. "I pulled out on time. Like I said, our finances are doing great." He hesitated before reluctantly adding, "We'll go over it tonight after dinner."

"There's something else. I am bored. I need to start working. I know you have this ridiculous notion that if I were married to someone from the Upper East Side, I wouldn't work. Well, you're wrong. I need something to keep my mind going."

"So you want to go back to running your store in the city?"

"Of course not. The girls love this place. I could open something small here-like the one I had in Paris."

Todd heaved a sigh of relief. "You know I'll support you if you want to go back to work. If that's what it'll take to make you happy."

"Yes, it is."

"Then I guess you're going back to work then."

"Good."

"Good."

And for the first time in a long time they smiled at each other-really smiled.

Later that night, after the kids had gone to bed, Katherine and Todd sat on the back porch reminiscing about old days. Katherine seemed more relaxed and carefree than she had in a long time and she didn't flinch when Todd reached out to take her hand in his. Maybe, she's coming around Todd thought.

After a while, Katherine shifted in her seat. "I think my feet are falling asleep," she swung the feet that had been tucked under her to ground.

"Why don't you stretch your legs out?"Todd suggested patting the seat.

Wincing Katherine twisted around gingerly swinging her feet onto wicker chair.

"You think a foot massage might help?"

"Ow, I don't think that's helping, " Katherine moaned a few seconds later pulling her pulling her leg away.

"Wait, just give it a minute," Todd said. Katherine straightened her legs again.

"One minute, that's all you get."

Katherine watched with a blank expression as Todd resumed rubbing her toes with his fingers. He did one leg and then moved on to the other. His hand moved to the crown of her foot, massaging it softly. Katherine watched Todd over the rim of her glass as she took another sip of wine. He brows furrowed in concentration as he worked his magic with his fingers.

"I cant believe you still remember how to do that," she said referring to the technique he had learnt in the massage class they had taken when she was pregnant with the twins.

"Well, I've had practice," Todd answered with a chuckle.

Katherine froze. "I'll bet you have" snapped rushing to her feet.

"Oh, no," Todd muttered knowing how his comment might have sounded to her. "I didn't mean it like that."

"I don't care. Just keep your hands to yourself and quit trying to seduce me." Katherine stormed off leaving Todd

I guess it's back to the guest bedroom for me again, he thought bitterly. For the rest of the week, Todd kept his hands to himself. Desperate to fix things between them, Todd printed out copies of their financial statements and went over it with Katherine. He pointed out that the house was completely paid for as was the apartment they kept in the city. The investments he had made in internet companies he made in college had made that possible. He also pointed that he'd started putting something aside for the girls.

Although they'd lost some money when the stock market crashed, they were still financially secure. They decided that it was only fair that Katherine invest her own money in the new store she was going to open.

Though he hated to admit it, he knew that Katherine was right. Money was an important aspect of marriage. They couldn't ignore their social and financial backgrounds-Katherine was rich, probably richer than he would ever be. It was fact. And it was something they needed to work around.

"You know, Steve's shipping out next week," Katherine said as they stretched out after their morning run.

"Yeah?"

"Yeah. My parents are having a going away party for him. I told them we'd be there with the kids. You think you can make it?"

"It'll be great to see the family again. It's been ages," Todd answered immediately. He waited knowing that there was something else Katherine wanted to ask him. Katherine had been edgy all morning, which was quite unusual for her. He held his breath.

"There's a charming little hotel not far from the country house," looked away concentrating on stretches. "We could spend the week end there after ... "

Todd's heart skipped a beat. Finally! He swooped her up his arms spinning her.

"Stop," Katherine squealed. "You're all sweaty."

Todd set her on her feet but didn't let her go. "You didn't let me finish. I saw going to say, we could spend the week end there provided that you're on your best behavior."

"Scout's honor. No more screw ups."

"There better not be." Katherine pushed him away, ran into the house and headed straight to the bathroom, her heart pounding in her chest. She could hardly wait for the week end to come. The past three weeks had been wonderful. He'd been every bit as attentive as he was when they'd started dating. He brought her flowers, took her and the kids out to dinner or to the park for picnics.

He cheated on you Katherine, she kept reminding herself over and over again. Although the fact that he had cheated on her still bothered her, Katherine was ready to forgive him and start over. She told herself it was the best thing for the girls, but deep down inside, she knew that that wasn't the only reason. She knew that she was a lost cause; she would never love anyone the way she loved Todd.

Chapter Fifteen

Todd couldn't believe how nervous he was. This is my wife for crying out loud, he kept reminding himself over and over again throughout the ride to the Johnson's country estate. Katherine, on the other hand was her usual cool self as she linked fingers with his for the better part of the drive.

He wanted the evening to be perfect for her. He had booked them the best room at the cottage Katherine had mentioned, had ordered flowers, scented candles for the bathroom and a bottle of chilled champagne and strawberries. He wanted the room to be filled with her favorite flowers and the bathroom, which held a large Jacuzzi to be full of scented candles. He had called twice to make sure, everything would be in place when they arrived.

"Katherine honey, are you ready to go?" Todd called out as he paced the room.

He glanced at his watch again. He was standing in Katherine's room at her parent's country estate waiting for her to finish getting ready so they could go downstairs and join the party.

"Hon, I'm growing roots here waiting for you," he called out again.

"Alright, alright, I'm done."

Todd's breath caught in his throat when Katherine walked out of the bathroom. She was wearing a beautifully-cut knee-length turquoise dress. The color looked great against her skin and bought out her eyes. Her hair fell loose around her shoulder in soft waves. She looked amazing and he was reminded of the first time they had met.

"How do I look?" she asked doing a little twirl. She knew that she looked great. The dress flattered her figure, emphasizing her great bust line and narrow waist. She'd taken longer than usual to get dressed and put on her makeup. The only jewelry she had on was the bracelet the twins had given her for her birthday.

It was a delicate white-gold bracelet with five charms. The tiny charms represented her favorite things. A dolphin, her favorite animal, the Eiffel tower representing Paris, her favorite city, a violin her favorite musical instrument, a little puppy to represent her Toby, the puppy her parents had given her when she was six and a heart which represented their love. Her friends would probably think it was tacky and her mother would raise an eyebrow, but Katherine didn't care.

Todd swallowed. "You look fine."

Katherine smiled. "Todd, you're holding your breath. I think I look more than just fine." she laughed. "You don't look so bad yourself," she added swatting him playfully. She let her gaze travel over him taking in the new suit and his slicked back hair. He looked so handsome and sophisticated and a little mysterious which she thought added to his appeal.

"I'm glad you approve," he said holding out an arm.

They smiled at each other and headed down to join the brunch.

Todd had a great time at the party. He couldn't seem to keep his hands off Katherine; he kept looking for excuses to touch her. He hogged her on the dance floor. It was their wedding reception all over again. When Steve asked him to join him and some of his army buddies for a "real drink", Todd instantly turned him down. He and Steve had always gotten along and he and his friends were lots of fun, but Todd did not want to leave his wife's side. "Come on, it'll be fun," Steve coaxed.

Todd's arm tightened around his wife's waist. "You know I'm not much of a drinker."

"Fine, then. We'll drink and you'll be the designated driver."

"Katherine and I kind of have dinner plans."

"We won't be out that long!"

"It's okay. You can come back for me in a couple of hours." She said quickly when she noticed the disappointed look in her brother's eyes.

"Are you sure?"Todd asked thinking of the large Jacuzzi.

"Of course," she said twisting to face him. "Just make sure you're back here before dinner. I'll make it up to you, I promise," she whispered kissing him on the lips.

"Don't worry, sis. I'll bring him back in one piece," Steve assured her with a huge grin.

Katherine was lying on her back on the couch in her father's den with her laptop on her stomach chatting with her friend online when she heard the front door open. She sighed as she glanced at her watch. At least Steve had brought him home on time.

As much as was looking forward to spending much needed quality time with her husband, Katherine had not wanted to disappoint her brother. He was leaving for war the next day after all and she had Todd for... well, forever, she reasoned. She had eaten so much for lunch, she wouldn't have minded missing dinner so long as they still had their big night.

She just hoped that Steve's buddies had not pressured Todd into drinking. The man had alcohol intolerance. A few shots and he was a goner. He was not one to back down on a dare either which made him, a bar and Steve's friends a very bad combination. Katherine shut down her laptop and got up. She bumped into her brother in the hallway.

"Hey, sis," he said looking guilty.

"You got him drunk didn't you?"

Steve tried to cover up a laugh with a cough. "I'm sorry..."

"Where is he?"

"He's in your old room. I told Nicole to stay with him while I get some coffee."

"It'll probably be better to let him sleep it off."

"Yeah. I'm sorry for ruining your plans."

"It's okay. I'm just glad you had fun even though it was at my husband's expense."

"It was kind of funny," Steve said chuckling.

Katherine narrowed her eyes. "Watch it!" she hissed punching his arm playfully.

"You know, you're getting a little cranky in your old age," he said.

"Just leave." She attempted to push him towards the door.

"I'm going, I'm going. I'm gonna get to the boys. Tell Nicole not to wait up," he said with a grin.

Katherine smiled as she walked up the stairs. It was good to see her brother laughing and being his playful self. He and Nicole must have ironed things out. She had been a little worried when she walked in on them earlier in the middle of what looked like a heated argument.

Nicole's face had been red with anger as she paced the room flinging accusations at him. Steve had just looked bored and unaffected by the tirade. She had never seen them at odds with one another, as far she knew they were desperately in love after five years together-something Nicole always felt the need to point out.

She did find it a little odd that her brother would choose to spend his last night drinking with his army buddies rather than with his wife. He's reporting to base tomorrow, not actually leaving, she reminded herself. Katherine tried to shake off the uneasy feeling as she made her way to find her drunken husband.

Chapter Sixteen

Katherine felt like she'd been kicked in the gut. She couldn't believe her eyes. She blinked again hoping that she was dreaming, but sure enough when she opened her eyes there it was... Todd and Nicole. Todd was lying on his back in the middle of the bed. Nicole was perched on the corner and leaning over him. They were kissing!

Shell-shocked, Katherine stumbled backwards bumped into a console as the bracelet on her wrist got caught on the shift dress she had changed into. She yanked her hand away oblivious to the pain and ran down the hall. She grabbed her purse where she had left in the study and headed out the door to the car, grateful that she hadn't bumped into anyone. Her hand trembled as she searched her purse for her car keys.

"You okay there?" Katherine turned around to see Uncle Paul's portly figure. Uncle Paul had been with the family since before Katherine and Steve were born. He had started out as a driver for father and had eventually become a personal assistant of some sort.

It was Uncle Paul who drove their mother to the hospital to deliver both her and her brother. For as long as she could remember, Uncle Paul had always been there. He was there at every family gathering-Sunday brunch, Christmas, thanksgiving, New Year. He and his wife sometimes joined them on family vacations. Katherine knew that Uncle Paul regarded her as the daughter he never had and to Katherine he was like the uncle she never had. no one had been surprised to see him teary-eyed during her wedding

"I thought you'd already left," Katherine managed, blinking back tears.

"I was watching the game with Mr. Johnson." Despite the years of convincing, Paul still refused to call his employer by his first name. "Everything alright?" he asked his eyes filling with concern.

Katherine shook her head miserably.

"Anything I can do?"

"Please Uncle Paul just take me home," she pleaded. Not one to ask questions, Paul took her hand and led her to his car, opened the door of the back seat and helped her in. He got in the driver's seat and started the car.

Katherine stared out the window in a state of shock. She felt as though she had walked into someone else's nightmare. Todd and Nicole? She still couldn't wrap her head around it. She felt numb. She didn't move or say anything for the hour forty-five minute drive.

"Katherine we're here. " Paul opened the door for her. Katherine's legs felt rubbery as she got out and walked to the door. "Thank you Uncle Paul," she said her voice sounding strange even to her ears.

"I'll be right here if you need me," he said pointing to the swing on the porch.

Katherine nodded. In a daze, she walked to the bedroom closet pulled out Todd's suitcases and began to pile his things in them. After filling three suitcases she dragged them down the stairs and out to the front porch. Paul knew better than to ask her any questions.

She dragged herself to her bedroom and collapsed on the bed, sobs heaving out of her chest. How could he? In her bedroom! In her parents' house! With her brother's wife! Wasn't he worried that she would walk in on them? Or her parents?! Or the kids? Or Steve?! Did he even care? How could he do that to her? To them? Steve loved him like a brother! And Nicole...!

What about everything that he had said? Did he even mean any of it or had they just been lies? Maybe he had been lying all along. Maybe really aws seeing someone in the city and that person was Nicole. Steve had been a way on tour a lot for past couple of years. Nicole could easily have been having an affair with Todd in the city and none would have been the wiser.

How long had this been going on? Why would he do that to her? How could he say he loved her hurt her in the worst way imaginable? And Nicole, who was like a sister to her, who had grown up with her building sand castles on the beach and fighting over toys in grade school. What was she thinking?

What had she done to deserve this? First Greg leaves her and now Todd. Todd, who said he loved her, who made her smile, whom she trusted above anyone else. How could he do this to her? How could they? Why? Katherine's mind reeled over the hows and whys. Her shoulders shook uncontrollably as the pain of the betrayal threatened to overwhelm her. Her heart felt like it had been shattered to a million pieces. She cried till her throat was hoarse and sleep finally took her.

Katherine was awakened by the sound of tires screeching to a stop. She knew immediately that it was Todd. All her pain and misery turning into anger, in a flash she got up and stomped down the hall from the bedroom to the landing at the top of the stairs. How dare he come here after what he had done? How dare he?! she thought her hands balling up into fists.

Todd had a vague memory of being carried out of the party and being laid down somewhere. He was not known for holding his liquor and tonight was no different. He hadn't meant to get drunk, just a few drinks to loosen him up. He thought about the special night he and Katherine had planned. He tried to get up but he it felt as though an elephant were sitting on him. "Oh, oh," he groaned over and over again as willed himself to get up.

He felt someone hovering over him. It must be Katherine, he thought. He reached out and pulled her towards him. All of a sudden his hands were pinned over his head as her soft lips descended on his. Through his drunken stupor he noticed that her kisses her more forceful and more demanding than usual. But then again, it had been a long time since they'd been together.

He pulled his hand from under hers and reached out to cup her face as he deepened the kiss. She made a sound of protest as she began to pull away. His eyes fly open clashing with a pair of beautiful brown eyes... not green, but brown. Todd pushed the stranger off him with more strength than he knew he possessed at the moment and sent her sprawling on the floor.

As he scrambled to sit up his drunken stupor immediately replaced with a cold feeling that chilled him to the bone. Nicole?! What the...?

All of a sudden, he felt sick. He got up and dragged himself to the bathroom where he threw up. Todd sat in the bathroom floor leaning against the wall and put his hands in his head. He tried to make sense of what had happened but he simply couldn't. Did Steve's wife just kiss him? Nicole? Impossible. Why?

Nicole had never done or said anything to suggest that she saw him as anything other than her bother-in-law and a good friend, but then again women were hard to read. Maybe it was something he never picked up on. He tried to think of what he might have done to encourage it.

As far as he knew, Steve and Nicole were happy and Nicole and Katherine as close as any two sisters could be. Todd got up and paced the bathroom. He needed to talk to Katherine although he was not sure if he would be able to bring himself to tell her what just happened. What would she say? Would she believe him? It was very unlikely; she was just beginning to let her guard down, to trust him. I just won't tell her, she doesn't need to know. No point in hurting her. Again. He would just have to confront Nicole about this. Whatever it was that just happened, it can never happen again.

Todd didn't know how long he was in the bathroom. By the time he got out Nicole had left which made him wonder whether the whole thing had been a nightmare. He grabbed his jacket and headed for the door trying to ignore the pound headache that was getting worse by the minute.

As he pulled the door shut behind him, he noticed a small figure of the Eiffel tower. His heart began to hammer in his chest as he bent down to pick it up. It was one of the charms from the bracelet the girls had given Katherine for her birthday last year. The bracelet was still on her wrist when he left. He remembered because she had been fingering the charms all night.

Could the charm have come loose and fallen off while he was still at the bar with Steve? Todd sure hoped so, but wretched feeling in his gut told him that that was unlikely. Todd searched the house for her. Most of the guests had already gone and the house was quiet. She wasn't in the den, she wasn't with the girls, she wasn't out in the garden or the kitchen... she was nowhere to be found.

He pulled his phone out his pocket. "Damn." Katherine wasn't picking up her phone. He tried again. And again. And again. When he tried for the third time, his call went directly to voice mail. Warning bells went off in his head. Katherine never switched off her phone.

Knowing that he was in no condition to drive, he shoved his car keys back in his pocket and called a cab. He would check the hotel first. Maybe she was there. Maybe she was in the shower and hadn't heard the phone ring. Maybe her battery had run out. Maybe, hopefully...

"I can't believe this is happening to me," he muttered to himself. He called the hotel twice. She was not there. Home, she has probably gone home. Knowing that it would be irresponsible to drive in the state he was in, Todd called a cab. He stomped into the house angrily to wait. His head was pounding and he felt like he was going to be sick again.

"What the hell was that?" he yelled at Nicole when he found her sitting alone in the kitchen looking miserable.

Nicole paled. "I'm sorry. I ...um... it dint mean anything. I was just trying to make Steve jealous."

"What?!"

"I didn't think. I'm ..."

"Do you know what this is?" he demanded holding the charm from Katherine's bracelet.

Nicole looked at the charm. She would recognize it anywhere. Why was ...? Nicole froze in horror. She remembered clearly that Katherine had been wearing the bracelet this evening. She had even teased her about it.

"That's right! It's from Katherine's bracelet. She probably saw us."

"M-maybe she dropped it earlier," Nicole stammered.

"Then why isn't she here? Or at the hotel? Why isn't she picking up her phone?!" reeling Todd gripped the counter for balance. Nicole reached for him to help him. "You stay the hell away from me," he ground out in a menacing voice.

They both started as Steve swooshed into the kitchen, "What's going on here?" Steve asked his eyes bouncing between the two of them.

Todd continued to glare at Nicole who was busy wringing her fingers, a tortured expression on her face.

"What the hell is going on?" Steve demanded all humor gone from his eyes.

"Why don't you ask your wife?" Todd said through clenched teeth and stumbled out the house.

Todd's heart froze when he saw the suitcases on the front porch. He opened the door quietly and saw Katherine standing at the top of the stairs. Her eyes were bloodshot red, her shoulders were shaking. It looked like her grip on the banister was the only thing that was holding her up.

"Please get out of my house, "she said in a calm voice.

"Katherine, it's ..."

"I said get the hell out of my house!" she screamed throwing a vase at him. The vase missed Todd by a hair and crashed into the wall behind him.

Todd didn't know what to say. How could explain himself when he wasn't fully sure of what had happened? But he had to calm her down. Todd held up his hands in the air and started slowly towards the stairs. She was shaking so much it scared the hell out of him. He had never seen her this.... this out of control.

Katherine kicked off her shoes and threw them at him, one after the other screaming, "Get out of my house. I never wanna see you again!"

Todd ducked and barely caught the second shoe before it hit him in the face. "Katherine please!"

"Get out! Get out! Get out!" she screamed at the top of her lungs.

"Son, I think you better leave." UnclePaul's quiet but firm voice came from the front door. "You can come back later, after she's calmed down."

Todd nodded. Tears stung the back of his eyes and threatened to spill out as he walked slowly to the car parked in the drive way. Uncle Paul took his suitcases and followed him with them, tossing them in the trunk.

Katherine crumpled to the floor as soon as Todd was out the door. Curling herself into the fetal position, she wept till she fell asleep. When she woke up, it was well past noon. She found herself lying in bed with the curtains drawn and a quilt draped over her. Her head throbbed and her eyelids felt heavy. Her brother was sitting by her, a worried look on his face. He was in his uniform.

"Hey, Kitty Kat," he said using the nickname he used for her when they were kids.

"Hey," she croaked. "What are you doing here?"

"Uncle Paul called."

"Oh."

"Are you okay?" he asked, his voice full of worry.

"I've had better days," Katherine replied with a short laugh that sounded false even to her ears. "I'm sure I look awful," she said sitting up and smoothing her hair. The last thing she needed was having him worry about her while he was going to war.

"You won't be winning any beauty pageants today, that's for sure," he said with a smile. His heart twisted at the sight of his little sister. She looked so small and vulnerable... broken, almost. He wished that he could stay and help her through this. She looked worse than she had after her break up with Greg and that had been pretty bad.

He felt like wringing Nicole's neck and he almost did after he had gotten Uncle Paul's frantic call. How could she be so stupid? Or selfish? And then she blames it all on him, claiming that he forced her into taking drastic actions. In a way Steve was glad he was leaving for Iraq. He needed to be away from her.

"Very funny," Katherine said trying to put up a brave face. "How long have you been here?"

Steve glanced at his watch. "A couple of hours," he lied. He didnt want to tell her that he had been there all night and that everyone had been sick with worry over her.

"Oh."

"Nicole told me what happened,"he began. As he had predicted, Katherine stiffened. "Todd..."

"Whatever it is you were gonna say, just please don't"

"Katherine, I know you're upset, but I think you should hear me out."

"No," she said firmly. "You are leaving today and the last thing I wanna do is argue with you."

"Katherine..."

"Steve, I said let it go. I mean it."

"Fine," he conceded, not wanting to rile her up again. "Tell me you will hear them out before making any decisions."

He reached over to touch her, she flinched. Katherine was surprised at the intense hatred she felt for her brother for siding with Nicole. "How can you even say that?" she hissed. "After what they've done to me?! To you?!!"

Steve felt guilty for dragging Katherine and Todd into their mess. He knew that Nicole was going to do something crazy, she'd been threatening to do so for the past couple of months. And he kept ignoring her. In a way, Nicole was right. He *was* partly to blame. After all, *he* was the one who had gotten Todd drunk in the first place. But that wasn't important right now. What was important was making things right. Katherine deserved to know the truth. She needed to know that Todd had nothing to do with the kiss she'd witnessed. "I think you should hear them out," he repeated.

"No."

"Katherine, you don't ... "

"I am not interested in anything either of them has to say."

111

"I had a feeling you would say that." Knowing that nothing he could say would make Katherine change her mind about listening to Todd or Nicole, Steve placed an envelop on the bedside table. Steve hoped that she wouldn't shred the letter before reading it. She would understand everything after reading it. One of the things he loved about his sister was her forgiving nature. She would be pissed off for a long while but she would eventually forgive them both. At least, that was what he was hoping.

Katherine ignored her brother *and* the letter pointedly. She didn't need to see it to know that it was from Nicole.

After a long silence, Steve asked brightly, "Got anything in that refrigerator of yours?"

Katherine was glad that he wasn't trying to ram the letter down her throat. "Are you ever not hungry?"

"No. Besides, I need to stock up on home cooked meals before I head off to war," he said with a grin. He held out a hand and Katherine took it climbing out of bed.

They went down to the kitchen where she piled Steve's plate with left overs. He wolfed his food down in an instant.

"What's the rush?" she asked.

"I have to head out, if I wanna make my flight."

She walked her brother to door and hugged him. "Oh, Steve, I wish you didn't have to go," she said holding him tighter. "I'll miss you."

"I'll miss you too Kitty Kat." he waited a beat then asked. "Would you do me a favor?"

"Of course. Anything."

"Please don't toss Nicole's letter."

Katherine lips tightened, her nostrils flaring out slightly in anger. That was exactly what she had been planning to do. She had been planning to shred it.

"Promise me," Steve insisted.

He doesn't want me to toss it, I won't toss it, but I won't read it either. "Fine, I promise."

Chapter Seventeen

Katherine spent the next two days in bed. She called her parents and told that she had come down with the flu and asked if the girls could stay for a little longer because she did not want them getting sick. She knew that her parents were aware that she and Todd were having problems-no doubt Uncle Paul or Steve had told them- and she was grateful for their feigned ignorance.

Certain that Todd or Nicole or both of them would keep calling her to apologize, she unplugged the house phone and switched off her mobile phone. When she wasn't shedding tears, she went running to rid herself of pent up anger. She couldn't bring herself to talk to anyone about what had happened; not Josh, not Ashley and certainly not her mother. She just was not ready. She missed her daughters terribly but she simply was not ready to face them yet nor was she ready to answer the questions she knew they would ask.

Katherine woke up on the third day resolved to get on with her life. The most important thing was to try and pull herself together and be there for her girls. The first thing to do, she decided, was to find a way to get Todd out of her system and out of her life for good. She went around the house with garbage bags grabbing everything that reminded her of him-pictures, paintings she knew he liked, books, dvds, cds, vinyl records, along with everything that belonged to him.

She even grabbed some of her things-perfumes, lingerie, cocktail dresses she knew he liked. By the time she was through she had filled up over a dozen garbage bags and her house looked like it had been raided. She hauled everything to the attic and went downstairs to survey her work. Looking around her she sighed. Even the furniture reminded her of Todd. She remembered how excited they had been when they gotten the house.

Rather than get a decorator, they had done everything together. She remembered how they would argue, make up and then laugh over it. It had been like a second honeymoon. Katherine shook her head trying to rid herself of the haunting memories. To keep from thinking about Todd and Nicole kissing-an imaged that had etched itself in her brain-she spent the entire night de-junking the house. The next morning, Katherine called her favorite charity organization.

"Ma'am, are you sure you'd like us to take everything?" one of the movers asked her pointing at the boxes lying in the garage floor.

"Yes. Actually, wait there's more." Katherine went to the linen closet and pulled out all the sheets for the master bedroom and along with towels and bathrobes. She then headed to the guest room and stripped the bed bare, trying to ignore the scent of Todd still clinging to the sheets.

"Here, you can take these too," she said dragging two garbage bags behind her.

By the time the movers left, the master bedroom was almost completely empty. This is exactly what my life is,

Katherine thought bitterly, empty. She sat on the floor in the middle of her bedroom and wept.

That night, Katherine slept in her daughters' bedroom.

The next morning, She set to work. She booked an appointment with a real estate agent and threw herself into setting up her floral store in the surburb. Patching things up with Todd was no longer an option for, but she wanted to make sure that whatever happened the twins lives changed as little as possible.

With a new project to keep her busy, Katherine decided that it was time she went to her parents to pick up the girls. The girls were disappointed not to see their father and it broke Katherine's heart to have to lie to them. She told them that he was on an important case and would come visit in his free time. She could not bring herself to tell them that their father had moved out-permanently.

"I was thinking of re-doing the guest chalet," Katherine's mother said as they sat in the garden of their country estate sipping tea. "You wouldn't mind packing up some of your brother's things, would you dear? I could have Maria do it, but you know how your brother hates it when people go through his things."

"Of course, mother."

After finishing her tea, Katherine headed out to the two-bedroom guest chalet at the far end of the garden. I don't understand why Mother insists of calling it the guest chalet. We haven't had any guest stay there for years. It should be called Steve's chalet, she mused. Steve had moved there when he turned 16 and used it whenever he visited.

Although, Steve hardly ever spent time in the country anymore, the place was littered with his things; trophies from high school football games, magazines, novels-lots of them-and CDs. Katherine quickly packed his things in boxes her mother-no doubt- had left there and headed to the bedroom feeling nostalgic.

She was going to miss her brother- she missed him already. She found the room had been cleared of Steve's things save one box. She carried the box out to the living room and flipped the lid open. There were several leather bound note books with Steve's initials on them; his journals. He'd always kept one, ever since they were kids. "In case I ever get famous," he'd say with a wink, "These will come in handy when I am putting together my memoirs."

There were several snap shots of her and Steve growing up together. Despite their two year gap, they'd always been close. They were inseparable all through high school. There were pictures of Steve and his platoon members in Iraq on his first tour. His parents had been furious with him for joining up and had wanted to use their connections to keep him from getting re-deployed, but Steve wouldn't hear of it.

"What's the point of being a doctor," he'd argued, "if you can't help people?" His mother pointed out that he could still help people from the safety of his private practice downtown New York, but Steve had already made up his mind and there was no stopping him.

115

There were also a lot pictures of him and Nicole on the slopes in Switzerland, eating with their hands in India, riding camels in the Middle East, on a Safari in Africa… so many pictures and in all of them they were smiling, their eyes shining with love. What happened to them? What happened to Nicole? Who could have guessed that sweet, kind-hearted Nicole would turn out to be a cold-hearted little slut?! She wondered gazing at the image of the pretty brunette.

"Hello."

Katherine nearly jumped out of her skin at the sound of the voice and the pictures she had been flipping through flying across the living room floor. Speak of the devil… she thought.

"I'm sorry. I didn't mean to startle you," said Nicole walking into the room slowly carrying a box. She put the box down on a table and approached Katherine.

"What are you doing here?" Katherine demanded her face going red.

"Emily told me you'd be here," Nicole said watching her closely, waiting for a reaction.

"I see," Katherine answered slowly, recovering her composure. Trust mother to try to get them to bury the hatchet. It had been almost a week since she last saw Nicole, but the level of hatred she felt had not abated one bit. "Why did you want to see me?"

"I wanted to explain things. It's not what it looked like,"Nicole said inching closer.

"It looked like you had your tongue down my husband's throat. But hey, for all I know you were giving him CPR."

"Please, you don't understand," Nicole pleaded.

"You're right. I don't understand. I don't understand how one of my best friends and not to mention my brother's wife could do this to me, could do this to my brother. No, I don't understand. Perhaps you can enlighten me."

Nicole looked at Katherine then at the pictures of her and her husband strewn all over the floor; memories of better days. She quickly picked up the pictures and placed them on the table face down. The thing she needed was a reminder of things lost…

Katherine sat down on the couch and crossed her legs, her eyes shooting daggers at Nicole. She was so angry, her head felt like it was about to explode. It was taking every ounce of her strength no reach over and throttle Nicole. "Well, I am listening." She motioned the other woman to sit across from her.

Nicole sat uncomfortably on the chair and took a deep breath. "Your brother and I had been having problems for the past year," she began. "The war, it changed Steve. He just wasn't the same anymore. He would stay up for

116

hours and when he would go to sleep, he would have these violent nightmares. He would wake up sweating and shaking..." tears welled up in Nicole's eyes.

"He wouldn't talk to me about it. I told him to see a therapist, someone that could help him, but he wouldn't listen. He said that I should stop nagging him. He started to sleep in the guestroom. And most of the time he acted like I wasn't even there."

Katherine hid her surprise. Her brother seemed perfectly fine to her. Every time she saw him, he looked happy and ... well. It was hard to imagine that Nicole was talking about the same person. Yet she knew that Nicole wasn't lying. She swallowed the lump that was beginning to form at her throat.

Nicole continued. "When you walked in on us that night, in the kitchen, we were fighting. I told him that things couldn't go on like that. I couldn't go on like that. I was lonely. He wasn't around most of the time and when he was he spent half his time at the clinic and the other half with his army bodies. We barely saw each other. You know what he said? He said he didn't care. I could do whatever I wanted. He couldn't care less." Nicole sniffed. She took a deep breath and continued. "I was hurt and angry. I want to get a reaction out of him. I needed to."

"And your way of doing that was to hurt *me*, to break up *my* family."

"Have you even listened to a word I said?! This isn't about you, Katherine," Nicole said angrily. "Steve hasn't been home for over six months. Before that he was gone another six months. And when he does come, it's as if he would rather be back there. He hasn't touched me in over a year. And if it took having to catch me kissing another man to jolt some sense into him, fine. I'd do it again in a heart beat."

Katherine shot to her feet. "How dare you?!" she shouted.

Nicole stood as well. "You're so busy being angry, you don't want to hear the truth," she shouted back. "Todd was drunk, he didn't know it was me he was kissing, not you. The minute he realized it he threw me off and went looking for you."

The two women stared at each other angrily. "Katherine the man loves you," Nicole said softly breaking the silence. "Don't push him away."

"You stay out of my marriage." Katherine said and walked out.

Katherine was so angry. She couldn't believe that her mother had ambushed her like that. She couldn't believe the nerve of Nicole. She was not even remorseful for what she had done. She did not understand why her mother was defending Nicole. It was possible that she didn't know that a back stabbing cheat Nicole was. She knew that her brother would never tell their mother about the incident.

But it still didn't make sense why he was defending Nicole for cheating on him with his sister's husband. True they were only kissing, but what if she hadn't got their on time, how far would it have gone? And what about Todd? He claimed to be sorry, claimed that he would do whatever it takes to fix their relationship... then he goes and makes out with her friend and sister-in-law on what was supposed to have been their big night. And now, Nicole claims that he thought it was Katherine.

A part of her wanted to believe Nicole. But being angry just seemed so much easier. Katherine decided not to think about it. She would just concentrate on the girls and setting up her business.

"Wow, Katherine. This is amazing," Ashley exclaimed as she looked around the partially decorated office. She was glad to see a few paintings from her gallery hanging in strategic places. "It's so ..."

"Different?" Ashley nodded.

"I know," Katherine said with a smile. "It's still a working progress though." It was modern and sophisticated with an urban edge to it.

"Well, the place looks great. Now, it's your turn."

"What's that supposed to mean?"

Ashley dragged her to the mirror in the hall way. "Katherine, you've had your hair the same way for over five years. I mean, it looks great and all, it could use a bit of a change as well."

"I guess I could use a new hair cut."

"I see you've lost about ten pounds-good for you."

Katherine rolled her eyes. "I wasn't exactly trying."

"You look fabulous that's all that matters and you're going to look even more fabulous after we've gone shopping." After a week spent seething at her nicole and at her mother for interfering, Katherine was more than happy to take on Ashley invitation to spend the weekend with her in the city.

"Are you ready to talk about it?" Ashley asked on the limo ride to the city. She had been out of the country for the past couple of weeks and felt guilty for not being there for her friend.

"It's a long story."

"It's a long ride," Ashley replied.

Katherine sighed and told her everything. "I am just so angry right now. I don't think I can talk to him or Nicole. Or my mother , for that matter."

"What are you going to do?"

"I don't know. I'm not sure. Todd keeps calling, but I don't think I can talk to him right now."

"Might be a good idea to hear him out."

"I can't. I just can't. I think I am through."

"You're not thinking of getting a divorce, are you?" Ashely asked alarmed at the resigned note in her friend's voice.

"I was. Now I am not so sure."

"Good, because that would be a big mistake. " Katherine ignored her friend and looked out the window. She still loved Todd, despite her best efforts to erase him from her mind, not to mention her heart.

Ashley knew her best friend well enough not to press the matter, so they sat through the rest of the ride in silence.

Ashley booked her an appointment with a celebrity hair stylist as well as a spa day. She did her best to cheer her up and for the most part it worked. By the end of the week end, Katherine did look fabulous, as her friend had promised- except for the sad look in her eyes.

"You look great," Ashley said as they walked out of Saks. It was a Sunday and they had just some back from another round of shopping. Ashley had made Katherine change into one of her new outfits. They dress brought out her eyes and flattered her spray tan. She had to admit the highlights and the haircut she'd gotten gave her a more youthful and sophisticated look.

"Thank you."

"I wish you didn't have to go back to the village," Ashley said with a pout.

"The suburbs is hardly is village." Katherine loved her friend, but honestly, the girl could be such a snob sometimes. She could still recall her friend's shocked expression when she told her that she was moving to the suburbs. Ashley had barely gotten over the fact that her friend was actually going to marry someone completely out of their social circle.

To Ashley, Todd was a hot a guy that would help her friend get over her heartbreak. She had not expected the relationship to last. She made no attempts to hide the fact that she thought Katherine was making a huge mistake by marrying "beneath her station". Over the years, she had grown to respect Todd and had to admit that her friend had made the right decision in marrying him.

"Keep telling yourself that, dear," Ashley retorted drily. "I was thinking... oh my god, don't turn around, but I think I just saw Greg."

"Who?"

"Greg. Your Greg."

"He's hardly my Greg, hasn't been for almost ten years. Anyway, with any luck, he won't see us."

"I don't think so. Looks like he's coming this way."

Katherine stiffened.

"Hello darling," the familiar voice said as he bent down to kiss Ashley on the cheek. "Seems like we keep running into one another these days, doesn't it?"

Ashley smiled. "It does, doesn't it?"

He turned to see who she was with, and his jaw dropped. "Why, hello Katherine," he said eyeing her with appreciation.

"Hello, Greg," she replied coolly. He looked exactly the same. Better, actually. He still had the easy grace and charisma Katherine had been drawn to the first time she met him. Looked like a filled out a little bit and he was sporting a nice, healthy tan.

"It's been a while hasn't it?"

"Yes it has."

Just then Ashley's phone rang. She shot Katherine an apologetic look and started to rummaged through the large Fendi purse she was carrying, searching for her phone.

"Let me help you with those," Greg said reaching for the bags Katherine was carrying.

"No, thank you. I can manage."

"It's really good to see you Katherine. You look great," his eyes sweeping over her once more.

"Thank you," she said.

"How have you been?"

"Great. You?"

"Great," he echoed. "It has been a while hasn't it?" he said after a beat.

"It has."

Katherine had often wondered how she'd feel if she ever bumped into Greg. She had also wondered if she would have forgiven him if he had pleaded long and hard enough. But that was before she met Todd. Todd had wiped out any thoughts she had about getting back together with Greg. In fact, he hasn't crossed her mind in years.

As she looked up at him, handsome and charming as ever, she marveled at the fact that he had absolutely no affect on her. she could feel his eyes roaming over her and yet she felt nothing.... Her blooding wasn't rushing in anticipation. Warm liquid heat wasn't spread across her lower abdomen. Her mouth hadn't gone dry and her knees had certainly not gone weak. She appreciate his beauty and charm the way one would a well kept garden. Katherine wasn't surprised that her attraction to him was dead and buried, but she *was* surprised to realize that she wasn't angry with him either. All she felt was mild curiosity as she return his gaze unperturbed.

"You know, I really wasn't happy with the way things ended between us," he said apologetically giving her a smile that once made her toes curl.

My brother gave you a black eye, what's there to be happy about? She thought smiling slightly.

"I wish things had been different. I hope there are no hard feelings," he said.

"None at all."

"I'm glad to hear that," he said. "Listen, I am only in town for a few days. Have dinner with me tonight. Let's catch up," he said in a voice that could melt butter.

"I don't think so."

"Come on, kitten," he said dropping his voice for effect. "It will be fun... like old times."

Katherine almost cringed at the memory of her turning goey every time he called her his kitten, his "very own kitten". "I can't," she said stiffly. "I'm married."

"So am I," he said lifting his left hand to show her his wedding band. She stared at the ring and then at him. "Remember how good we were together," he added. The voice she had once found irresistible, now the voice just irritated her. She couldn't believe that she had spent almost a year pining over him! The man was such a sleazeball who clearly had no respect for the sanctity of marriage! Katherine was glad he had left her. He had done her a huge favor.

"I remember," she said.

Greg smiled licking his lips. The sight revolted her.

"And you know what, Greg?" She reached over and snatched her shopping bags from him. "I've had better." His head snapped back as if she'd just slapped him across the face and he looked at her with shocked eyes. It was obvious that he still believed that he had the same hold over her as he did several years ago.

He straightened quickly, his eyes darting around to see if anyone had heard her. "Suit yourself," he said with a shrug but she could see the effort behind the smile. Greg hated rejection.

"And thank you," she said.

"Whatever for?"

"For stopping me from making the biggest mistake in my life," she said walked away feeling better than she had in a weeks.

"What was that?" Ashley said when she caught up with her. "Greg was as red as a lobster."

"I know," Katherine said with a laugh.

Chapter Eighteen

Katherine was still riding on a strange and jittery when she got home. She was glad she had run into Greg. She hadn't thought about him in years, but seeing him made her realize how low she had been willing to settle for. The ironic thing was that she had known all along that he was unfaithful to her. She had feigned ignorance because she thought that she would never find anyone she was as passionate about or who was as passionate about her. She had been willing to move to Dubai with him and to marry him.

She had been so willing to forgive him, but not Todd. Todd who had been honest with her about his affair. Todd who had tried to apologize to her with tears in his eyes. Nicole is right, I am being selfish, she thought. I should at least given him a chance to explain. Nicole too.

With the girls spending the day with their father, the house was so quiet. She picked up the thriller she'd been reading and settled down in the living room couch. As riveting as the story line was, Katherine couldn't concentrate on the words. Her mind kept drifting back to her confrontation with Nicole.

She thought about the letter Steve had brought with him the day he came to say good bye. The letter she had vowed never to read but couldn't bring herself to get rid of. She went to her closet and reached for a box she had put the letter in and ripped the envelop open. With a sigh, she sat down on the window seat and began to read.

By the time she was through with the three-page letter, her anger had dissolved. She had not idea what her brother had been going through. Nicole was right, she had been selfish. She had been so involved in her problems that she never considered how hard the war had been on her brother. Steve had always been her rock, and now to think that he had been in so much pain and she was not there for him broke her heart.

She thought about the e-mails they exchanged or their chats on Skype and… if she had looked closer she would have noticed that something was amiss. He seemed quieter than usual, less engaging but Katherine hadn't thought much of it. She had been too busy wallowing in self pity.

She picked up the phone and called her friend. Nicole picked on the first ring. "Katherine?"

"Yeah."

"Katherine I am so sorry … "

"Nicole, why didn't you tell me? About Steve, I mean?"

"I wanted to. Really I did. Steve made me promise not to say anything. Things were so bad between us, I was scared that if I said anything, he would leave me."

"But he looked so happy when I saw him."

"For the most part he was, it's just hat he gets these bouts of depression. And I guess I kept hoping that things

123

would get better."

"I still wish you had said something. We would have been there for you. I could have talked to him. Done something."

She heard Nicole sigh.

"How's he doing now?"

"He's doing better, I think. I think this might be his last tour."

"I know. I am glad. I get so scared every time he leaves."

"Me too. I think things are going to be different now. We had a long talk after... um... well, before he left and I think things are going to get better."

"I'm glad."

"Me too." She was silent. "I really am sorry about Todd."

"That's okay."

"I didn't mean to hurt you."

"I know."

"I know, it's none of my business. But Todd loves you."

Katherine sighed. "I know."

"He thought it was you. He was drunk."

"I know. That man cannot hold his liquor at all. It's embarrassing," Katherine retorted in an attempt to lighten mood.

"I noticed."

They both laughed.

Kyla and Debbie squealed as Todd pushed them on the swings. He missed them terribly. He missed his wife terribly. He had been ecstatic when received the text message from Katherine asking him to pick the girls. He had been hoping to see her, but Gladys informed him that she was in the city. He noticed how she'd transformed the house, their house in such a short time. She had gotten rid of the paintings they had bought together in Paris, the little souvenirs from their trips and all of his pictures.

As he walked around the living room, he could not find any picture of him in the entire house. It was as though he had been erased. The transformation was unsettling. He knew how conscious Katherine was about her environment. Was she trying to erase him from her life? Was she thinking of a fresh start?

Todd didn't know what to think. Katherine was the most unpredictable woman he had ever met. Even after almost a decade together, she still surprised him. The past week had been so difficult, so lonely. He refused to go back to the city despite the messages and calls he'd been receiving from his partners.

The long lonely nights gave him a chance to do a lot of soul searching. He thought about his life and how different it was from what he had imagined it would be. He had always dreamt of being a successful lawyer. He also dreamt of having a family, a close knit family. The kind of family he had before his parents had gotten killed in the car accident.

He thought that making partner at a prestigious law firm and marrying the girl of his dreams would make the dream come through but it hadn't. He realized that he hated his job. He was grateful for the financial security he enjoyed, but the work left him feeling empty. He had invested so much time helping expand the business that he had forgotten why he wanted to be a lawyer in the first place. All he did was find ways to make the rich richer.

It's time to shift gears, he said to himself. He would dissolve his partnership with the law firm and register a new practice, a practice that helped people for a change. He tried to imagine what it would be like to open his practice in the suburbs and found that he liked the idea. Very much. Business would be slow, but it wasn't like he needed the money. He had invested wisely in telecoms businesses in Africa and computer companies in the east, he was assured a steady income that could more than support their lifestyle.

His phone beeped. Another text message from Nicole. He had not replied her text massages, emails or phones for the past three weeks, but the woman still would not give up. In his noble manner, Steve had apologized on her behalf, shouldering the blame for her inappropriate behavior.

Todd could identify with Nicole. There was nothing worse was than having someone you love freeze you out. He could understand the fear that would lead one to act irrationally just to get a reaction, any reaction. However much he understood her predicament; he still could not bring himself to forgive her.

Steve had told him that the thought of Nicole kissing another man had jolted him back to reality. He realized that if he didn't stop pushing her, he would end up losing her for good. While their marriage was on the mend, his and Katherine's was destroyed probably for good.

Katherine was a very proud and stubborn woman and he doubted that she would give either one a chance to explain what had really happened that night. Todd's finger paused over the delete button. How could he accuse Katherine of being unforgiving when he was guilty of the same thing? Maybe it was time he gave Nicole a chance. He opened the text message to read her apology and froze. He couldn't believe his eyes. It was the best thing he'd heard all week. *Explained everything to Katherine. I think she understands now. Good luck!*

"It's time to go home," he called out to the girls.

"Ice-cream first," Kyla said.

"Yes. Daddy you promised."

"Pleeeeeeeeeeeeease!" they said in unison.

"Alright, but we don't want to be late."

Todd couldn't contain his excitement as he walked to the front door with his daughters. Maybe now, Katherine would agree to see him. He was disappointed when Gladys, not Katherine let them in. "Is she home?" he asked.

"Yes, she came in not too long ago," Gladys said with a smile.

"Please let her know that I'm here,"

Todd walked around the kitchen enjoying the familiar scent of freshly baked bread. Gladys came back looking uncomfortable. "She's sleeping."

"Oh," Todd said trying to keep the disappointment from his voice.

"Does that mean you're leaving?" Kyla asked with a pout.

"Do you really have to go back to the city, Daddy?" Debbie whined.

"It's just for a little while," he said bending down to hug his daughters.

Discouraged, Todd drove aimless for a while dreading going back his miserable hotel room. He should have known that it wouldn't be this easy. It was obvious that Katherine didn't want anything to do with him. He would give her space. It would kill him to do it, but he would try.

Katherine was awakened by the sound of her daughters jumping on her bed. "Mommy, mommy, we're back!" they sang in unison. "We missed you mommy," they said smothering her with kisses.

"I missed you too," she said with a laugh. "Did you girls have fun?"

"Yeah loads of fun."

"Heaps and heaps of fun," Debbie chipped in an effort not to be outdone.

"Is your father still downstairs?"

"He left," Kyla said sulking.

126

"He asked if you were home and then he said he had to go back to the city," Debbie informed her.

"I see." He hadn't even attempted to see her. What if he's gotten tired of trying to apologize? Katherine was afraid that maybe she'd gone too far. What if she had finally pushed him away?

"I miss daddy," Debbie pouted.

"So do I, honey, so do I."

Throughout the entire drive to her parents' country estate, Katherine contemplated whether or not she should call Todd. It wasn't until after she had put the girls to bed that she decided.... yes, she would call him. She picked up her phone and started to punch in his number when a grief-stricken Emily appeared in the doorway.

"She is gone," the older woman said simply. Aunt Margret had been battling breast cancer for the past few years. Katherine remembered how shocked she had been when she had returned from Paris to find Aunt Margret in the hospital. She had barely recognized her. Margret 's bumbling infectious enthusiasm was gone. The humorous glint in her eyes was replaced with that of pain. The chemotherapy had weakened her. She had also lost most of her thick auburn hair with streaks of gray here and there in what had been left of it. Eventually she had shaved what was left of it and had taken to wearing a wig.

For a while, the future seemed bleak; but then a miracle happened. Margret went into remission. And for almost five years, she was fine. Her hair grew back and so did her strength. She went back to being the Aunt Margret they all knew and loved.

Last Thanksgiving, she found a lump in her other breast. The doctors told her that the cancer had spread and there was little they could for her. Despite the pain she was in, Aunt Margret put up a brave face. She was a source of strength for all of them. And now she was gone. Katherine crossed the room on shaky legs to hug her mother.

Katherine still couldn't believe it when she woke up the next morning. She couldn't believe that the Margret she had known and loved for years was gone. They all knew that this day was coming. But Katherine was still reeling with shock. Katherine opened her closet and pulled out a dress she hadn't worn in years. It was a black crepe knee-length dress with a demure neckline. There was so much to be done and Katherine knew that she couldn't allow herself to break down, at least not yet. She had to think of the twins, her mother and Uncle Paul. She felt sorrow wash over her as she thought of Paul. She couldn't even begin to imagine what he was feeling.

With shaky fingers, Katherine picked up her mobile phone. *Todd, I need you, she typed.*

Chapter Nineteen

Todd's heart was pounding so hard he thought his chest was going to explode. He had not seen Katherine in since that terrible night. She never replied any his emails, or returned his phone calls. All his attempts to get a word across to her through her friends, parents or even the nanny had been futile. He had even given of hope of hearing from her till he saw her text message. He couldn't believe it. His eyes misted over as he read the four words over and over again. Four beautiful words he had lost hope of ever hearing from her again.

Todd wandered around the house looking for Katherine. He couldn't believe that Aunt Margret was gone. His heart wrenched at the thought of how devastated Katherine must be. He knew how close Katherine had been to her. There were so many people at the house that it took him a while to find her. She was sitting in the garden her head with her feet tucked under her, and her head resting on Ashley's shoulder. Her eyes were closed and her hair fell loose about her shoulder. When Ashley noticed Todd, she gave Katherine a little nudge.

Katherine straightened. "I'll be inside if you need me," her friend gave her hand a reassuring squeeze and walked into the house.

"Hello Katherine."

"Hello."

"How are you holding up?" Katherine shrugged. He noticed that she was thinner and her hair was lighter and shorter, falling about her shoulders in different layers. Even with the anguished look in her face, she looked beautiful.

"Do you want to talk about it?" he asked softly as he sat down next to her.

Not trusting her voice Katherine smiled and shook her head . She knew that he would be there and she had been sure that she was ready to face him, but not anymore. Seeing him, unleashed all of the emotions she had been trying all morning to hold under reigns. All she wanted to do was to run into his arms, bury her face in his chest and hide. She was glad he didn't touch her because she would have lost it. He understood her well enough to know not to do that.

"Do you want to take a walk?" he asked after a while.

Katherine nodded. They walked in silence.

"How are things going with the new store?" he asked breaking the silence.

"Great," she answered. Again grateful that he understood that the last thing she wanted to talk about was Margret.

"That's great. It's always made you happy, I'm sorry I made you give it up."

Katherine looked at him in surprise-it was the first time he had actually admitted it. She noticed that he too had lost weight and it looked like he hadn't had his hair cut in weeks. She had always preferred his hair that way. That was the way he had it when they'd first met. "What about you?" she asked. "What have you been up to?"

"I dissolved my partnership with the law firm."

"Really?" she was shocked.

"I'm thinking of opening something small, closer to home."

Katherine flinched at the word "home".

Todd noticed stopped walking. "Katherine, I am so sorry. Not just about Nicole. About everything. I am so sorry for the pain I've caused you. I'm sorry for hurting you and the girls. I love you Katherine. I hope you can find it in your heart to forgive me."

"Love was never really our problem, Todd," she said taking two steps before stopping. They both fell silent, thinking about the things they'd been through over the past couple of years. Even though the silence was killing him inside, he would just have to tough it out till she was ready to forgive him if ever.

"I suppose you will be going back later," she said. Even though her voice was steady, he could tell that she was fighting back tears.

"I thought I might stay till tomorrow if," Todd replied with a sinking sensation. "If you want me to that is," he added cautiously.

He saw her take a deep breath before turning slowly to face him. She regarded him calmly and smoothed her dress. Todd held his breath. He had a foreboding feeling that he was not going to like what she had to say next. He was right.

"There is no need for that, really," Katherine answered. Todd felt the earth shift from under him. He opened his mouth to plead, apologize, say something, but nothing came out. When he saw her text message he had hope that it meant she was ready to give him another chance. Again. Apparently, he was wrong. It had been her grief talking. He shoved his hands in his pockets. She didn't have to see that they were trembling. If he was going to go out, he was at least going to go out like a man.

He simply nodded and slowly. "This is very confusing for the twins. They're devastated. It would be nice to have you," Katherine added. Todd felt weak with relief. He felt a lump form in his throat as he looked at his as she shifted her weight from one leg to another. "Todd, I'm really glad you're here," she added.

Todd closed the space between them, pulling his wife into a tight embrace. Katherine wrapped her arms round him and he knew that he had been forgiven. "I'm really glad I'm here too," he whispered into her hair as tears of happiness rolled down his face.

THE END

Zeitfracht Medien GmbH
Ferdinand-Jühlke-Straße 7
99095 Erfurt, Deutschland
produktsicherheit@kolibri360.de

Druck:
CPI Druckdienstleistungen GmbH
im Auftrag der
Zeitfracht Medien GmbH
Ein Unternehmen der Zeitfracht - Gruppe
Ferdinand-Jühlke-Str. 7
99095 Erfurt